What the critics are saying...

"The sexual is so thick; you would need a knife to cut it." ~ *Just Erotic Reviews*

"In Her Nature is a spicy love story that any paranormal romance lover will find captivating and arousing. Well-done job to author, Lorie O'Clare!" ~ *eCataRomance Reviews*

"In Her Nature 'a hot and spicy read'." ~*The Road to Romance*

IN HER NATURE

Lorie O'Clare

IN HER NATURE
An Ellora's Cave Publication, December 2004

Ellora's Cave Publishing, Inc.
1337 Commerce Drive Suite #13
Stow, Ohio 44224

ISBN # 1419951742
Other available formats: ISBN MS Reader (LIT), Adobe (PDF),
Rocketbook (RB), Mobipocket (PRC) & HTML

Edited by: *Briana St. James*
Cover art by: *Syneca*

Warning:

The following material contains graphic sexual content meant for mature readers. *In Her Nature* has been rated *E-rotic* by a minimum of three independent reviewers.

Ellora's Cave Publishing offers three levels of Romantica™ reading entertainment: S (S-ensuous), E (E-rotic), and X (X-treme).

S-*ensuous* love scenes are explicit and leave nothing to the imagination.

E-*rotic* love scenes are explicit, leave nothing to the imagination, and are high in volume per the overall word count. In addition, some E-rated titles might contain fantasy material that some readers find objectionable, such as bondage, submission, same sex encounters, forced seductions, etc. E-rated titles are the most graphic titles we carry; it is common, for instance, for an author to use words such as "fucking", "cock", "pussy", etc., within their work of literature.

X-*treme* titles differ from E-rated titles only in plot premise and storyline execution. Unlike E-rated titles, stories designated with the letter X tend to contain controversial subject matter not for the faint of heart.

Also by Author:

IN HER NATURE

Chapter One

Tall field grass lay flattened from many tire tracks, leaving darkened, curvy trails across the open field. Several rows of cars had parked in the isolated area. The ground was damp, and the air too. Moisture clung to everything, weighing down scents, keeping them lingering longer than necessary. And it was cold, too damned cold.

Simone DeBeaux climbed out of the backseat of the pale blue Suburban, searching the group of people who moved around the parked cars, congregating in the field with a quiet reluctance.

None of us want to be here, she thought, sensing the silent acceptance that seemed to blanket everyone's mood.

The smell of coffee and exhaust clung to the cold air, trapped in the moist stillness of the late afternoon. Wet earth and leather mingled with the scents, and Simone gulped in the aromas as she took a deep breath and shut the car door.

I dare any of you to confront me, she silently challenged the pack. The field was isolated, the forest thick around them, venting the cold air and the smell of pine. She didn't know who owned the land, but guessed one of the Rousseaus had kept it in the family since their burial ground was here. Not good for humans to be lingering around a werewolf graveyard.

Rich greens, muted by clouds into darker shades, spread out before her. British Columbia was a piece of heaven in its beauty, and she would have relished it, were it not for the somber reason that drew the pack together.

There were familiar faces; she had anticipated that. She had grown up with these werewolves, and they were her pack, whether she liked any of them or not.

But tradition ran deep in their blood. Tradition and respect for rank never dwindled, not among her kind, not among the *lunewulf*. Not among any werewolf pack.

She moved slowly around the parked cars, in no hurry to mingle with the growing group that hovered over their coffee, poured from thermoses brought with them. Everyone here viewed her as one man's slut, and she doubted any of her actions today would change that opinion. Werewolves were slow in changing their views.

She stared at the man in front of her who strolled with calm confidence into the group ahead of them. Johann Rousseau didn't acknowledge anyone as he passed pack members they had both grown up with. Simone stared at his backside. Long muscular legs, with blue jeans hugging them, and a perfectly hard ass once had been a distraction she couldn't resist. Snakeskin cowboy boots added to his rugged appearance. His plaid, down jacket drew in around his waist, accenting broad shoulders. She let her gaze drift up him, to blond curls that fell to his collar. She knew firsthand how soft those curls were.

If she didn't stay with him, the group who parted to let him pass would close in around her. She would be left on the outer edge, alone among her pack members. Johann wouldn't turn around to make sure she remained with him. He had probably forgotten all about her by now, even though he'd brought her with him to this Godforsaken event.

His thoughts wouldn't be focused on what the others thought of their presence here together today. He had a ceremony to conduct. She didn't have that luxury. Her thoughts were free to wander since she was simply an idle spectator, here to give her last respects, of which she had none, to the deceased.

"There she is," someone said, and heads turned in her direction.

Simone flinched, ready to stand her ground if confronted, until she realized that the group now surrounding her stared, and began pointing at something behind her.

She watched Johann turn around, but like the others, he didn't focus on her either. He did, however, turn his attention to the bitch standing next to him. Simone focused on her, too.

Samantha Rousseau, Johann's new mate, turned around slowly, her knitted cap pulled over her ears and bleached blonde hair sticking out around her neck. Her hand slid to her protruding belly, where Johann's cub grew. The older bitches might question that Johann had taken Samantha out of honor and duty since she was obviously so pregnant, and the mating was new, but Simone knew Johann had mated with Samantha out of love. It showed in how they looked at each other.

Even in her extra-large flannel shirt, Samantha looked beautiful, her face glowing from the cold air, and her long thin legs accented by her snug jeans. Her gaze was wary though, and Simone caught the worried glance she gave Johann.

But Johann had already looked away. He left Samantha's side and walked toward an approaching vehicle.

"That's her," someone murmured next to Simone.

"It's the whole lot of them," someone else said.

"Well you know they would all turn out today."

Simone listened to the comments of the people around her, while the tension grew in the crowd. No one liked the old bitch.

Several men opened the back of the Expedition, which had parked on the edge of the rows of cars in the field. And although she didn't know all of the immediate family, she guessed they were all Rousseaus. Simone moved to stand next to Samantha, and the two of them watched the group of men lift a long, narrow coffin from the back of the sports utility vehicle. Others from the pack helped two older people out of the front of the car, but Simone didn't focus on them.

Four men carried the coffin toward the group, which parted to allow them to walk through the field. Simone gave each man her attention in turn. Johann was one of the men, his expression solemn. She didn't know the other three men, but one of them stood taller than the rest, catching her eye.

"Look at that hunk." She nodded toward him, keeping her tone a soft whisper.

"Are you talking about Johann?" Samantha glanced at her, before returning her attention to the solemn procession.

"Fuck Johann." Simone stared at the man who now passed by them. He stood a good six inches taller than

Simone, yet she was pretty sure he was purebred, or he sure wouldn't be here.

"You better not fuck Johann," Samantha whispered back.

Simone glanced at Samantha. "You have nothing to worry about. Look at the guy in the back." Simone knew her past experiences with Johann would always bother Samantha. But there was nothing she could do about it. "He's head and shoulders taller than the other *lunewulf*."

"You know he wouldn't be here if he wasn't purebred." Samantha turned her gaze to watch the men as they placed the coffin on to the platform that would lower it into the hole dug out below. "I wouldn't be allowed here if I wasn't Johann's mate. I'm lucky no one has thrown a fit that I'm not pure *lunewulf*."

"If you want to call it luck."

Samantha nodded her agreement.

Simone watched the men move to the side as the coffin was lowered into place. The strong scent of freshly dug dirt for the grave filled the air, mixed with the rich smell of the grass in the field, and the sweet odors filtering from the pines surrounding them. None of it could hide the tension that mingled around her. The smell of emotions was thick in the group of werewolves, and it made her uneasy.

Although she couldn't remember having been to a burial ceremony before, she knew what to expect, and moved with Samantha when the pack formed a circle around the burial site. A ring not to be broken, representing the strength of the pack.

The man who had caught her eye stood to the side of the grave, and Simone noticed he didn't appear to have a mate standing with him. Hopefully that meant he was single. She grinned inwardly, hardly paying attention to the ancient words that Johann uttered as the ceremony began.

"As it was with our ancestors, and will be with our descendents." Johann's words garbled over his extended teeth, his body partially changed, showing respect in both of his forms, werewolf and human.

Several elders stepped forward, each carrying a gold goblet. The man who had caught her eye helped carry a large cauldron into the middle of the circle. The elders dipped their goblets into the cauldron, the dark red fluid flowing from the base of the ornate chalice. An older woman, dressed like the natives of the surrounding timber country, in a thick corduroy dress with white wool stockings, approached with a sacramental cloth, and dried each goblet.

"We drink from the blood of the heart, offering sanctuary to the soul of our departed, Kathryn Rousseau." Johann's voice rang crisp across the field, and Simone felt a chill from the breeze. "We create a road of blood for Grandmother Rousseau to travel."

The tall blond remained by the cauldron, and she took a moment to enjoy his perfectly sculpted body. He didn't wear a coat, and his button-down flannel shirt was untucked from his jeans. He was obviously ready for the ceremony to end. She planned to enjoy the view of him stripping in the field when they all changed into their fur. She wanted to know if he was as fine-tuned as his stance suggested.

"It better not be cold," Samantha muttered, and the two of them turned their attention to the goblet that was being passed toward them. "I might puke if it is."

Simone stifled a chuckle, but agreed that cold blood tasted nasty. "I'm sure they drained a doe right before the ceremony," she reassured her friend, and could already tell from its rich fragrance, as the cup drew nearer, that the blood was fresh.

"Drink from the blood of the cauldron," Johann was saying. "We unite as a pack, sharing our grief as we do our kill."

Simone doubted too many people grieved the death of their previous pack leader. She glanced toward the tall blond and realized he watched her. Or did he focus on Samantha? Simone knew her friend was quite the looker, even in her pregnant state. Not to mention that she was a curiosity since Johann, a native of the area, had just returned home to be pack leader with his new pregnant mate.

But either way, the man looked in her direction, and Simone couldn't help but offer a small grin. His jawbone flexed—a small smile appearing. He was looking at her, and she had never seen deeper pools of blue than she did when she stared into his eyes.

She let her gaze graze over the man, taking in his thick broad shoulders, blond hair that curled with glimpses of red, and a close shaven beard. He seemed too tall, too big, too much werewolf to be *lunewulf*. Although Johann was a good-sized man, and several others in the pack were as well, this man stood several inches taller, built like a lumberjack. His shirt stretched across his chest, bulges rippling under the material.

He would be an aggressive lover, Simone decided— her favorite kind. The man seemed to pin her with his gaze, pinning her so that she couldn't move. Would he be the kind of werewolf who enjoyed capturing his lover like he would his prey? The cold air didn't bother her any more, as yearning traveled through her, a smoldering beginning low in her gut, and growing in intensity as it moved between her legs.

"Here," Samantha whispered, nudging her.

The sun moved slowly behind a cloud in the gray sky, the air growing chillier while she sipped the tepid blood from the goblet. The thick fluid ran smoothly down her throat, bringing the beast within her to life. The hairs prickled on her back as she passed the large cup to the person next to her. She would dance the dance of death tonight, under the warmth of the white moon.

And would the tall stranger dance with her? She watched him help the others carry the large cauldron back toward the cars. The leftover blood would be drained later, and the cauldron cleaned. Simone watched muscles move under his shirt as he carried the heavy, oversized pot.

The ache in her pussy grew hot. She wanted this man, but how to go about getting him when Johann had her under lock and key.

"As it is written, so it shall be." Johann read from a large book that one of the elder Rousseaus held open for him. "I claim leadership of the *lunewulf* pack, founded by the Rousseau family, who moved here with the development of Fort Saint James, and have hunted, worked, and raised cubs on this land for over a century. Does anyone challenge me as pack leader?"

Simone glanced around the group, as the others did as well, waiting to see if anyone would challenge Johann as pack leader. The question was part of the ceremony, and she knew Johann wasn't worried about being challenged.

The tall, sexy stranger walked into the group, after having secured the cauldron next to the SUV. Several heads turned his direction, and Simone watched him too, his expression impossible to read with his short cut beard masking him, and the shadows from the late afternoon sun highlighting the contours of his face.

The smell of tension drifted through the cool, damp air though, alerting her as it seemed to do those around her. Silence loomed throughout the field, the lingering scent of blood being replaced by another, more dominating scent. Hairs prickled down her neck, and then traced icy patterns along her back, mixing with the heated desire that staring at the stranger had brought on.

Was there a challenger? She glanced at Samantha, and then over at Johann. Trepidation seemed to ripple through the group, and she wasn't sure, but it seemed heads turned toward the tall sexy blond. He stood along the edge of the circle, staring at Johann, and either not noticing that more than several pack members had given him their attention, or not caring.

The stranger didn't speak, and crossed his arms over his massive chest, a silent indication that he feared no aggression, or that he had no intention of challenging Johann. She didn't know for sure what his body language meant.

Johann cleared his throat, gathering everyone's attention back to him. He obviously interpreted the large man's gesture as non-aggressive.

"We bury our dead as our ancestors did," Johann said. They had reached the end of the ceremony. Thank God.

A stir began through the group assembled. Simone glanced up to see Johann shed his jacket, and then unbutton his shirt. She turned her head to search for the tall blond who had held her attention. He had stood along the edge of the group a second before, but now was gone.

Her fingers stumbled over the buttons on her shirt while she turned to look for the stranger. Well hell. There might have been some pleasure to this boring funeral after all, had she been able to watch the tall, well-built blond strip.

People around her took off their clothes, dropping to all fours when the change consumed them. The tension in the air changed, the stillness no longer thick with a sense of duty and boredom. Instinct took over, bones stretched, skin thickened to hides, and fur covered skin.

Within minutes werewolves filled the field, a final tribute during a funeral, the beast within all of them surfacing.

Simone strained to find the stranger, dismay clouding her senses when she couldn't find him. She pulled her shirt off, the chilled air attacking her nipples painfully. The tightening surged through her and her human soul held on, preventing the change as denied lust consumed her. Disappointment ran through her when she realized the stranger had disappeared, and she dropped to all fours.

White werewolves, their glossy coats the color of the moon, with thick heads and jowls that housed long, pointy fangs, with sleek, red tongues, filled the remote field. A fearsome sight, had there been any humans present to see the transformation, but this was a private affair, and a tradition maintained through centuries. They honored their dead in human form, and then in their werewolf form.

Samantha nudged against Simone, her middle protruding with her cub, and the swell of her nipples visible through the fur on her belly. Samantha was a brave bitch; she would give her that. Many here had strong convictions about mixed breed werewolves, and Samantha had been shunned before for not being purebred.

The dark silver streaks in her white coat made her beautiful, Simone thought, and she kissed Samantha's cheek, running her long tongue against her friend's sleek coat. *I won't let them hurt you.*

But when she looked toward the group, ready for anyone who would challenge Samantha's presence, she realized the two of them were not the focus of anyone's attention. She spotted Johann immediately, not too far from them, as if he had been heading toward them, but he didn't focus on them either.

The *lunewulf* pack danced uneasily, moving around each other, nonverbally sending a message of ill ease. She glanced around, not understanding, wondering what kept the pack at a standstill when she had assumed they would begin a run.

Then she spotted them. Behind her, staring warily at the rest of the group, were five very large werewolves. All of them had the glossy white coat of the *lunewulf*, but the group of them dwarfed the rest of the pack.

Now why did that sexy hunk move behind her when he changed to a werewolf? At least he got an eyeful!

Even in her fur, the air turned colder, giving her a chill as it breathed off the forest of pines. The sun seemed to disappear, leaving them in shadows. The foul scent of prejudice filled the air, and Samantha backed up behind her and sat down, obviously protecting her unborn cub.

Simone paced in a circle in front of her friend, unsure of the history but keenly aware that for some reason, these five weren't welcome.

Johann turned his back to the five, an obvious statement in itself that he didn't fear them. He paced back and forth in front of his pack, the pack that had just accepted him as leader, and then lunged, snapping at the paws of several of the werewolves in the group.

I will say whom we shun from now on! His bark was more of a growl as he sneered at the pack members, who backed away from his bared teeth. No one would challenge Johann. None of them wanted to stand out and state their inbred distaste for anyone who didn't look just like them.

Johann lunged at the group, his bark a ferocious howling growl that cut through the growing twilight and echoed through the trees surrounding them. No one stopped him, and all parted quickly, then took off with the infamous speed the *lunewulf* were known for.

Simone fell into line with the group, long claws ripping at the earth as they headed for the hills, the ceremonial run of death that concluded the end of every funeral. They would run to celebrate life, and allow parting for the dead.

One of you is my tall, sexy stud. She glanced to the edge of the group, where the larger werewolves pounded the earth, keeping pace with the group, muscles rippling through their fur as their long legs stretched.

And from across the group, one of them turned and met her gaze, silvery blue eyes laughing at her as a predator would his prey. He broke from his group of buddies, and she watched as he avoided others in the group, and moved in on her. Simone's heartbeat raced, and she began panting as instinct consumed her, and the desire to mate fogged her senses.

You can't fuck the wolf during a public run, her rational thought told her.

On the other side of her, Samantha yelped, and Simone turned to see what had happened to her friend. Before she could focus, something rammed into her, and she fell head over paws over the rough terrain.

Chapter Two

"I'm fine," she said, for what seemed like the fifth time, and ground the Suburban into second gear as she slowed to the speed limit.

They entered Prince George, having left Johann with other men from the pack to secure Grandmother Rousseau's grave.

"Johann didn't have to bulldoze into you like that." Samantha sat in the passenger seat scowling.

"I was supposed to be watching out for you." She couldn't have agreed with Samantha more. And she would have told Johann a thing or two about his treatment of Samantha if the entire pack hadn't been watching.

But right now, all she wanted to do was calm Samantha down. She didn't like seeing her friend so upset, and wanted Samantha reassured that she could take care of herself.

"I don't need a babysitter." Samantha hit the car door with her fist.

She slowed to the speed limit. They passed a few of her old stomping ground hangouts, which she would have pointed out to Samantha if her friend hadn't been so upset.

"How were you supposed to know that I got a cramp?" Samantha continued, fuming over the matter. "I shouldn't have been running so fast, I guess."

"It's okay." Simone stared at an old warehouse that used to be a nightclub she had frequented years ago.

Memories trickled through her of fucking Johann behind that building one night, but she pushed it out of her head. "I'm not hurt, and you're not hurt. Johann is just feeling his oats about being a new pack leader. I have no doubts that you and I can file his teeth down a bit."

"He slammed into you because you were drooling over that oversized werewolf," Samantha spat out. "He can't claim both of us. I won't have it. I don't care if everyone around here has three mates. Johann will have one mate, and so will I!"

She worked to remember the order of the streets, allowing the Suburban to creep down the quiet road. She turned onto the street of the babysitter who had watched all the cubs during the funeral.

"Do you want to stay in the car?" She looked over at Samantha, who seemed focused on the people in the yard.

"Our cub will have lots of pack mates his or her own age," Samantha mused. She rubbed her tummy, while staring out the window at pack members and their cubs lingering in the front yard. "No. I'm queen bitch now. I can't be hiding in a damned car."

Other than those mingling in front of Babette Trent's house, the dark neighborhood was quiet. She remembered Mrs. Trent, or Babs as the other bitches called her, as being an uptight fuddy-duddy when she was a child. As an adult, Babs had always stuck her nose in the air whenever Simone saw her, and walked the other direction. Simone had always thought the old woman had a nasty smell about her, even as a werewolf. More than once she had thought the smell was due to the fact that the old woman probably hadn't been laid in over forty years. She had been a widow as long as Simone could remember.

They got out of the car and started toward the house, when a small blonde child bolted toward them.

"I hate them, Mommy!" Jere Rousseau, Simone's daughter, ran toward them, her blonde curls bouncing around her head.

"If that old bitch laid one hand on my daughter..." she said under her breath.

"You know she didn't," Samantha assured her. "Jere is Johann's daughter. They will respect her as the pack leader's cub."

She hated the fact that Jere would be known as a bastard cub. But for now, she couldn't do anything about it.

"Who do you hate?" Her daughter ran to her, but then Jere turned and bolted back toward the yard.

"What the hell was that all about?" Samantha asked while the two women walked toward the group still mingling in the yard.

"There you are," an older, disapproving voice said.

Simone recognized old Babs the second she saw her. The bitch hadn't changed a bit in the past few years. The stocky woman marched toward Simone, her scent preceding her.

"You need to get that daughter of yours in line if you expect to enroll her in school next year," old Babs said in a form of greeting.

"It's good to see you again too." Simone couldn't help but add a sultry tone to her greeting.

Babs ignored her comment and turned her attention to Samantha. Simone wasn't sure she had ever seen the old bitch smile before, but Babs' expression changed notably when she reached out to take Samantha's arm.

"We are all dying to meet you, hon." Babs displayed a row of yellow teeth when she smiled, and Simone thought for sure her cheeks would crack when they wrinkled into creased lines.

Samantha was dragged away, and Simone knew she should go with her to make sure those old bitches treated her with respect. But her daughter was into mischief somewhere, and she needed to find her. A pang of sympathy ran through her as Samantha went off to perform the duties of her title and be surrounded by the nauseating stale odor of a bunch of old women.

Turning, she looked for Jere, and spotted her on the edge of the yard, being dragged toward the street by two oversized brutes who had to be at least seven or eight years old. Sure, her daughter would receive lots of respect as the pack leader's daughter. She groaned, and went over to rescue her daughter.

"Someone better teach you some manners," she growled at the two cubs.

To her surprise, the two boys tried to grab Jere out of her hands.

"She needs to learn manners, too," the older of the two said.

Simone pulled her daughter to her side when Jere tried to lunge at the two boys, and then bent over so that she was in the boys' faces.

"You keep your hands off of my daughter." She allowed the change to take over enough to make her teeth grow. "Or it will be me who teaches you two little mutts a thing or two."

"They are hardly mutts." A baritone voice from behind her brought Simone to quick attention.

She started to turn around, but stopped to secure her grasp on her daughter when Jere tried to pull one of the boys' hair.

"To the truck," the man behind her said. "Both of you, move it now!"

Simone looked up into the face of the man she had drooled over at the funeral. And she did have to look up. He was huge! She had seen tall men before, but this sex god standing before her had arms so thick she was sure she couldn't wrap her fingers around them if she used both hands. His chest had to be thicker than a beer barrel; there would be no way she could wrap her arms around him and clasp her hands together behind him. Muscles strained the material of his shirt, and she imagined him strong enough to lift and move a car if he wanted. She had never seen a man so well-built. Her insides lit with fire at the thought of tumbling with this wolf in the meadow. With a man this big, all she would be able to do would be to climb on and enjoy the ride.

But her daughter's small hand in hers forced her to curb those thoughts, and she tilted her head back to look at his face.

Deep blue eyes glistened in the night, and made her forget what she was going to say. Never before had she seen such perfection in a man. As huge as he was, and as tall as he was, he didn't seem intimidating—more like enticing.

He pointed his finger at her, tapping the tip of her nose. "You must not be accustomed to the wild side of boy cubs."

She couldn't help but notice how long and thick his fingers were. She almost held her hand out to compare, but she would swear his index finger was longer than her palm. How thick and long would that make his cock?

Jere backed behind her legs.

"They were dragging my daughter across the yard." She wondered how he would look if he smiled. "That is hardly appropriate behavior."

She didn't have to wait long to find out. Beautifully straight white teeth appeared when he grinned. "They must like her."

Simone's heart skipped a beat. Her mouth seemed too dry to respond, while her mind conjured pictures of him dragging her across the yard. "Is that the example you give them?" she managed to ask, and was proud of herself for not blushing.

"I only drag the ones that I want really bad." He had lowered his voice to a husky whisper.

The sound of it sent chills racing through her, but her skin grew hot against the cold night air. He raised his hand toward the side of her head, as if he might actually grab her hair and pull her along with him.

"Simone! To the car now!" The order sprang through the darkness, and she looked past the giant in front of her to search for Johann, who had just yelled at her.

"Mommy. Let's go." Jere tugged at her pant leg.

She reached for Jere's hand, and stepped around the sexy stranger when she spotted Johann with Samantha. Johann scowled at her, and Samantha didn't look pleased. The last thing she wanted was a scene in front of old Babs' house. She didn't have a choice about living in this town, and she didn't want the community given cause to badmouth her when she hadn't done anything wrong.

Long fingers snaked through her hair, and she froze when he palmed the side of her head. He didn't pull on her hair, but simply held her head stationary.

Jere's hand slipped out of hers, and she watched her daughter run over to Johann.

"Does he own you?" He moved close to her and had lowered his head so that he could whisper in her ear. His scent made her legs feel like vanilla pudding. He had a rich smell of pine about him, and the crisp clean aroma of freshly cut wood.

"No," she whispered, daring to stare into those aqua blue eyes.

"Then why does he command you?" His hand moved through her hair, turning her face toward his.

"I...I have his daughter." She searched his expression for disapproval, but found none.

Instead, he seemed to digest this information, and straightened, focusing on Johann for a minute, before looking down at her again.

"I will have you." He stared down at her with eyes that seemed to glaze to a dark sapphire. His expression appeared serious; he wasn't playing with her. Was he?

His male scent thickened the air around them, and her body reacted to it, humidity soaring in her pussy.

No man had ever left her at a loss for words before. Could this man be more brazen than she?

"Is there a problem here?" Johann spoke from behind her, breaking the spell the tall stranger had placed her under.

She turned to look at Johann, and the man let his hand slide from her head.

"I heard you. I'm coming." And that wasn't an understatement, she thought, as she felt the dampness in between her legs turn into a soaked pool of lust.

The rich, sweet smell of their desire didn't leave the air around them in a hurry, and she knew Johann inhaled it deeply. As pack leader, he could dictate on behalf of her wellbeing; but damnit all to hell, if he was going to prevent her from having a good time.

Johann took her by the arm, and started her walking toward the car. She noticed Samantha helping Jere into the car, and then glanced at Johann in time to see him give a reprimanding glare to the man who had just shattered her insides like no other man had ever done before—not even Johann. She didn't dare look over her shoulder to see what the huge stranger's reaction to such a punishing look might have been.

* * * * *

Jere's curls were damp as they sprayed over the little girl's pillow. Her daughter breathed deeply and slowly, her face the calm softness of a child sleeping and content. Simone leaned over and kissed her on the forehead, the scent of strawberry bubble bath lingering on her clean skin.

She had made many bad choices in her life. There had been some wild werewolves, and she'd blown all gossip about her behavior to the wind. Other pack members' opinion of her never bothered her much. But this little girl, sleeping in the bed the two of them would share for a while, was not a mistake or a bad choice.

Granted, having Johann's daughter tied her to him. And for years she would have loved the opportunity to share his den, be with him, ached for him to come to her. But now Samantha was in the picture, and she carried his cub. They were cut from the same cloth, outcasts in a way, never the one to quite measure up in the eyes of others, and both willing to take the world on by the teeth.

"Sleep well, princess," Simone whispered.

She stood and lowered the window, shutting out the fresh scent of pine and the cold night air.

"Settling in for the night?" Johann sat in the kitchen, with a cordless phone, cell phone, and several papers spread out before him on the kitchen table.

She had given thought to a late night run, maybe to see if she could find her tall, sexy hunk, but she wouldn't say that to Johann.

"I might take a run before I crash for the night." That wasn't completely a lie.

"I won't have you running around by yourself. It's not proper." Johann let his gaze amble down her, and Simone couldn't tell whether he looked at her with disgust or interest.

Samantha is your mate now, my dear. She had a right to find someone, too.

"It never bothered you before that I ran by myself. Don't turn righteous on me now," she snapped at him.

Johann slid the chair back and stood up. His flannel shirt was untucked, held closed by only a few buttons at the bottom , creating a long V-shape view of his dark blond curls that covered well-sculpted chest muscles.

"I am pack leader." He wagged his finger at her. "And I won't have you out running with just anyone."

"I wasn't planning on running with just anyone." She walked away from him, not in the mood for his pompous attitude. "Don't let being pack leader give you a big head. You don't own me." She wanted to ask him why he sent her flying during the running ceremony earlier, but knew she had already pushed his limits from the anger that clouded the room.

Grabbing her boots, she plopped down on the couch. Samantha strolled down the hall, her hair damp and one of Johann's T-shirts hanging to her thighs. She looked cute with her long legs and bare feet, and damp hair hanging like raw silk to her neck.

"I have final say over you, and any other unclaimed bitch in this pack. I don't think I need to quote pack law to you." Johann stormed into the living room, stopping when he saw Samantha.

She slipped her feet into her boots, trying to keep her fingers from shaking. If she showed fear, he would attack. Instincts ran strong in werewolves. "You don't need to raise your voice. Jere is sleeping."

Johann lunged at her, and she jumped over the coffee table and grabbed Samantha, using her as a human shield.

"Don't you play righteous mommy with me," he growled, his teeth noticeably longer, and his blue eyes burning with a silver hue. "I know about your past. Don't you ever forget that."

"I did the best I could for her." Her heart raced, and as much as she hated to admit it to herself, she hated Johann getting mad at her. "I raised her all by myself."

"That wasn't my fault." Johann reached for Samantha, and pulled her to the side, so that she no longer blocked his path to Simone.

"You two really shouldn't fight about this," Samantha said, and held on to Johann's arm.

"You're right." She smiled at Samantha, and then turned toward the door. "I'm going out."

"Where do you think you are going?" Johann was right behind her.

"I don't know." She shrugged, and reached for the door handle. Blood pumped through her and she fought to remain calm, not wanting him to smell fear or concern on her. "Maybe I will check out our old stomping grounds."

"You'll stay away from that Cariboo *lunewulf*." Johann grabbed her arm, and swung her around to face him. "If I hear one word about you running with any of them…"

Her sex god was a Cariboo *lunewulf*? She had never met one of the rare species of werewolf, but had heard rumors of how dangerous they could be.

"Well now, isn't this interesting?" She glared at him, forcing herself to ignore the hard grip he held on her arm. "At the funeral you seemed to make it quite clear that you wouldn't have them shunned. Will you keep the nasty reputation of *lunewulves* being prejudiced alive in your pack, Johann?"

"I have no prejudice toward them." His tone softened, as did his grip, and his expression relaxed. He took on the manner of a father explaining something to his cub. She hated it when he talked to her like this. "They are hard-working werewolves, just a bit on the wild side." He let go of her arm, and then tapped his finger under her chin. "And those are the last type of people you need to run with. I'm merely looking out for your best interests, which is something you should be concerned about, too."

She relaxed her stance as well, offering him a smile that she didn't wish to give. She felt like smacking him.

"Fine then. I'll just go down to Murphy's and see how the town has held up in my absence." That was the last thing she wanted to do, but held her ground, and hoped Johann couldn't tell she was lying.

"And what about Jere?" Johann grabbed her arm, ready to stop her from opening the door. "You would just leave her without a sitter?"

She yanked her arm free and pulled the door open, the cold night air and rich scent of pine immediately surrounding them.

"Of course not. I don't have to worry about a sitter. She is with her daddy." She hurried out the door before he could stop her, and pulled it shut behind her, inhaling the cold air in an attempt to slow her pounding heart.

Chapter Three

Johann stared at the front door, frustration surging through him, and the crisp night air still lingering around him. The phone rang, and he turned in time to see Samantha watching him before she turned and walked into the kitchen to answer it.

"It's for you," she said, and he saw the worry in her eyes.

He smiled, taking the phone, and knew somehow he needed to assure his mate that she had nothing to worry about when it came to Simone. If he had wanted her for a mate, he could have had her. Samantha needed to learn that she was his mate by his choice. Simone had his daughter, and therefore would learn to show a respectable image of herself, even if he had to beat the sense into the bitch.

"This is Johann." He reached for Samantha, when she would have walked out of the kitchen, and pulled her backside to him, smelling her damp hair, and feeling her soft rear press against him. Maybe fucking his sexy mate would wipe the worry from her.

"Johann. I'm sorry to bother you at a late hour." An older man spoke at the other end of the line. "My name is Roger Pembroke. We haven't officially met yet."

He didn't recognize the name, and knew he would need to focus on getting to know his pack members.

"It's good to meet you." He hoped he sounded chivalrous. "What can I do for you?"

"My concern could have waited until the next pack meeting, but I've been made aware of a few things and wondered if I couldn't stop by briefly."

The last thing he wanted right now was company. Samantha felt real good in his arms, and his cock already ached to be inside her.

But this was the life of a pack leader, and both of them would need to get accustomed to it.

"Of course you can, if it's important." He thought he hid his disappointment, but saw it mirrored at him when Samantha turned in his arms and looked up at him. "Do you know where we live?"

"Sure do. Not too far from me and the Mrs.," Roger Pembroke told him. "I helped get your place ready for you and your family."

"Well you did a real good job." He ran his fingers down Samantha's cheek, and she smiled up at him, her soft brown eyes full of questions. He combed his fingers into her hair and pulled her head toward him, taking in her sweet smell. Her scent was like an aphrodisiac, changing daily with her pregnancy. He loved it. "When can we expect you?"

Roger Pembroke told him he would be right over.

"We're going to have company," he told her, holding her to him and placing the phone on the table behind her. "But I would much rather fuck you until you begged me to stop."

Samantha giggled into his chest, and he ran his hands down her back, then slid them underneath her T-shirt.

"Johann?" Samantha had a hard time concentrating with his hands spreading her ass. The cool air that rushed up to her moist pussy did nothing to put out the fire that smoldered there.

But she had to ask him. She had to know before anyone showed up at the house. It was hard saying how long he would have company, and she didn't think she would be able to fall asleep wondering why he seemed so obsessed with Simone.

He ran his hands under her shirt, his flesh hot against her skin. Her womb tightened under his touch, and he brushed his head against hers, until she looked up at him, then his mouth covered hers.

"Yes?" he breathed into her, and then impaled her mouth with his tongue.

God. She wanted him to fuck her. But was this his way of avoiding the questions he suspected she would ask?

He moved one hand to her ass, pressing her to him, butterflies springing to life inside her, as his other hand grabbed her breast and squeezed. Instantly, she ached for him to suck her nipples, their sensitivity growing daily with her pregnancy.

His mouth left hers and trailed kisses to her ear. He nibbled at her lobe and sent shivers racing through her. Suddenly it was difficult to focus on her questions, and she knew that was what he wanted.

"Why did you tell Simone to stay away from that werewolf?" she asked, before all rational thought left her.

"All he wants is a piece of tail," he whispered into her ear, and then bit her neck.

Her insides spasmed, an explosion of molten heat and liquid fire racing through her. She grabbed his shirt, a moan escaping her instead of a response to his statement. Her pussy swelled, demanding his attention.

"Maybe that is what she wants too," she managed to gasp, and then cried out when he pinched her sensitive nipple.

"Do you really want to talk about Simone?" He moved his face so that it was mere inches from hers, looking down at her.

She struggled to focus as desire rippled through her, racking her senses, filling the air around them with the rich smell of her cum.

"I want…" She wanted to know that he didn't want to keep Simone for himself. A knock on the door caused her to pause.

Johann kissed her quickly. "To be continued," he said, and then pushed her to arm's length. "Get yourself to bed, unless you want to get some clothes on and entertain our company with me."

"I'll stay up with you." She forced strength back into her wobbly legs so that she could stand without leaning against him.

Johann smiled, then turned her around and slapped her rear. "Good. Go get dressed."

He took a moment to compose himself, ordering his cock to put current matters at hand. Taking his time, he strolled to the front door.

"We're sorry to intrude on your family time." Roger Pembroke stood in the middle of the living room with two other men behind him.

He took a minute to introduce the two, Aaron Steppling and Jordan Rousseau, a distant relative, although Johann wasn't sure of the lineage offhand.

"We've come to talk to you about the Cariboo *lunewulf*," Jordan cut in.

"Now, now." Roger held his hand out, silencing Jordan Rousseau, who looked a bit disgruntled by the action. Roger ignored the man's irritation. "Johann, we understand that you grew up here, but have been away for a few years. All of us agree that our pack should be more open-minded, and not frown upon strangers."

Roger paused, and gave Jordan a cutting look. Johann watched the three men as they apparently struggled with whatever it was they had to say. Samantha returned to the living room, still in his T-shirt, but now with sweatpants on as well. Her cheeks were flushed a flattering rose color, making her brown eyes brighter. She was stunning.

But he guessed she had overheard the comment about the pack being more open-minded, and he knew she was sensitive about not being pure *lunewulf*.

He stepped around the men, and held his hand out to her. Her timid smile about undid him, and she placed her hand in his.

"Gentlemen, allow me to introduce my mate, Samantha Rousseau."

"I'll get some coffee going." Samantha gestured to the upright brown couch housed along the wall. "Please have a seat."

A minute later, two of the men sat on the couch, Jordan Rousseau paced in front of them, and Johann leaned in the doorway to the kitchen, the rich smell of coffee slowly penetrating the room as Samantha made herself busy behind him.

"So tell me your concerns about the Cariboo *lunewulf*," he prompted them. "Surely they all haven't done something wrong."

Roger Pembroke sat on the couch. He pulled his ball cap, which advertised a local woodshop, off his head and began wringing it in his hands.

"No. No. It's nothing like that. They're hard-working people," Roger began.

"Just like the rest of us," Aaron Steppling added and sat at the other end of the couch while watching Jordan pace.

"We came over here to tell you about Rock Toubec." Jordan Rousseau stopped pacing. "You know that was his land we were on today." Jordan was tall and thin, with small eyes that narrowed in on whoever he spoke to. He seemed to be harboring a few emotions that Johann couldn't quite sniff out.

"What land?" Johann asked.

"The Rousseau graveyard," Jordan told him, and the two men on the couch both shuffled a bit, as if suddenly uncomfortable.

"Toubec paid the back taxes on it and pulled it right out from under the Rousseau name," Aaron said.

Jordan stopped pacing and crossed his arms over his narrow chest, staring at Johann as if waiting for his reaction.

"When did this happen?" Johann had so much to learn in order to be a good pack leader. He had no idea the Rousseau land wasn't owned by a Rousseau anymore. The last he heard, the Rousseaus owned a good twelve hundred acres, forty parcels about, of good land north of Prince George. "And who is Rock Toubec?"

"Toubec is that Neanderthal who was sniffing around your..." Jordan Rousseau paused when Samantha entered the living room with two mugs of coffee in her hands.

"Around his what?" Samantha handed one of the mugs to Jordan Rousseau, and then turned and gave the other one to him.

Johann could smell her anger.

She turned and walked past him into the kitchen and returned with two more mugs. Aaron and Roger accepted the cups, and then she stood in the middle of the room, crossing her arms over her protruding belly.

"Go on, Mr. Rousseau. You were saying?" She turned her bright brown eyes on to the thin gentleman, and Johann hid a smile at the man's obvious nervousness. His bitch would be one to reckon with; he liked that.

Roger Pembroke cleared his throat, then slapped his legs and stood up. The other two men in the room gave him their attention, and a sense of hesitation settled on everyone. He turned his attention to Johann, and looked serious.

"You haven't been home in a while and we want to bring you up-to-date on some facts," Roger said, and the other two men nodded their agreement.

"Go ahead." He pulled Samantha against him.

She hesitated at first, then allowed herself to stand with his arm around her waist. The three men in the room watched the interaction.

"Rock Toubec bought the Rousseau Ranch a little over a year ago. After that, a handful of Cariboo *lunewulf* moved to town. He was the first to approach Grandmother

Rousseau about joining the pack, and since he was a major landowner..." Roger explained.

"And started contributing to all of her favorite charities," Aaron added.

Roger nodded. "She allowed him to join the pack. And made it a statement that we approved of all purebred *lunewulf.*"

Samantha snorted, and the three men shifted uneasily.

"Sorry, miss." Roger began wringing his hat again. "But there is something you need to know about Toubec. We feel it's our duty to tell you."

"Your, umm, friend could be in trouble," Aaron said.

Roger held up his hand to silence the man, and Jordan began pacing behind Johann and Samantha.

"There are some rumors about Rock Toubec, and they merit your attention." Roger paused, and when he realized he had everyone's attention, he continued. "The wolf has two cubs, and rumor has it that his mate died a nasty death at the hands of some American mutt werewolves."

Samantha stiffened in Johann's grip, and he tightened his arm around her. It would take time to get the pack accustomed to her mixed heritage, but now wasn't the time to press it.

"Rumor has it that she was pulled out of a run one night when she was out with some other bitches, raped, beaten and left for dead by these Americans," Roger continued. "Now this happened back when Toubec still lived in the mountains, and they say the pain of it made him leave his home pack and find a new life."

"That's when he came here and took Rousseau land." Jordan cut in.

"That's a terrible thing to have happen to the wolf," he said quietly. "But you say these are just rumors?"

"We're pretty sure of their accuracy," Roger told him. "I guess no one has called for a report from his old pack on it."

"Never had reason to," Aaron added, and sipped at his coffee.

"But here is where the rumor turns nasty." Roger focused on Samantha, and his expression softened. "I beg your pardon for discussing matters like this in front of you, ma'am."

"You said you were concerned about Simone," Samantha prompted. "Is she in trouble?"

He knew she fought to sound calm in front of these men, but liked the aggressive side she could show if need be.

"How does it turn nasty?"

"In the year that Toubec has been here, a few bitches have strayed out his way from our pack. He has bruised up a few of them, and sent them running. Rumor has it that he has a vengeance to settle, and that he might take it out on someone with American associations." Roger paused again, and looked at his hat that he had twisted in his hand. "I'm not going to beat around the bush here. I don't know what your personal relationship is with Simone Rousseau, but we all know she has your cub. And it's common knowledge you got her staying here with you. Now you bring home an American mate, and we all saw Toubec sniffing around Simone earlier. The possibility exists that she might be in danger."

"Do you think Toubec would attack Simone because I've got American werewolf blood in me?" Samantha sounded like the thought was preposterous.

"Ma'am, you don't know these mountain werewolves. They have a different mindset." Roger sounded like he was apologizing.

"Johann," Jordan said. "She's a Rousseau. She isn't claimed. And she runs a bit too wild. Toubec may take the initiative to take some pent-up anger out on her if she gets too close. We all keep our bitches clear of the man. It's common knowledge we don't have enough of them to let them stray."

The thick pungent scent of fear filled the room. Samantha pulled away from Johann and crossed her arms over the bulge in her tummy. She turned and looked up at him, and he saw that her brown eyes had turned moist.

"Go make sure she is okay," she told him quietly, and that was all he needed to hear.

※ ※ ※ ※ ※

Simone didn't really feel like checking out any of the local bars. No one in the pack had caught her eye, other than her big sex god, and he had cubs.

More than likely he is at home, she thought, and resigned herself to the fact that she would just get a good run in, and enjoy the open spaces.

She took off around the back side of the small ranch house, and headed north, enjoying the thick scent of pine, and allowing it to help clear her head of the unpleasant conversation she had with Johann.

The wolf wouldn't bully her around now just because he had some rank. She would make that quite clear to him.

The change rippled through her, and she fell to all fours, then started off at a slow trot until she had cleared the dense pines behind the house.

Open fields appeared before her. The rich scent of dirt, and fresh smell of prairie grass filled her nostrils. Blood pumped through her with the eagerness of her breed, bred to run, and claim the wild that surrounded her.

Would she enjoy a fresh kill this evening? That might be what she needed. A wonderful cock to take the edge off would be nice, but she doubted at this point that she would find any tonight. And not just any werewolf would suit her this evening. She had a taste for a large Cariboo *lunewulf*, but she had no idea where to find him.

Northern geese flew over her, their honking filling the night air as they called out to each other. She let out a howling bark, silencing them so that only their flapping wings could be heard as they hurried from the deadly predator warning she had issued. *I command the night tonight.*

Several foxes darted away from her off to the side of the field, not wishing to be the focus of her entertainment for the evening. She laughed into the cold night air, relishing her superiority over the wild, and decided to stretch her muscles a bit before deciding what would be her kill.

Her night vision excelled in wolf form, and the black outline of a barbed wired fence grabbed her attention. She cleared it, soaring through the air as her muscles tightened and flexed under her skin, and felt earth tear under her claws as she landed in the meadow on the other side.

Her gallop turned to a sprint, and the open area allowed her to give speed to her run, shredding the ground beneath her with the pounding of her paws, and lapping at the crisp air as it slapped her face.

This was rancher's land. The change in the scents around her let her know cattle were nearby or had been recently. Although fresh beef was a prime kill, she respected other's property, and pack law. Killing owned animals was forbidden.

The smell of fresh water tickled her nose, and she slowed her gait, then veered toward the source. A large pond, rippling silently against the night breeze, appeared before her, and Simone walked through the tall grass fencing it in, and then drank the cold water. Fish swam through the depths. Her ears perked at the sound of them, muffled as their fins moved through the dark abyss before her.

Everything around her remained silent. Too silent it dawned on her. She straightened, her muzzle wet from the water, and glanced around at the quiet meadow. No birds sang. No animals scurried through the underbrush. Nothing moved. The breeze even seemed to have stilled.

Her hackles went up as she backed away from the water, realizing too late that she wasn't alone in the meadow.

Chapter Four

The scent of another werewolf grabbed her attention.

She moved backward slowly, instinct having her hug the ground, while she searched the area for the source that heightened her senses.

At the edge of the meadow, shadowed by surrounding trees, a large werewolf stood motionless. She couldn't tell from the distance if she had been spotted, but knew if she could smell them then they could smell her.

Johann's words about running by herself ran through her mind. He would have her hide if word got out that she was out here by herself. A good fuck in the meadow was always fun, but she knew how men loved to talk.

She shook the thought from her head. He wouldn't control her. She wouldn't let him.

The large werewolf entered the meadow, moving slowly, and she realized then that it was a Cariboo werewolf. The beast almost doubled her in size, massive shoulder blades moving under a glossy white coat as its head lowered to the ground.

It's sniffing me out.

Fear and excitement danced inside of her. She had no idea if this was her sex god or not. She had seen five of them at the funeral, and didn't know how many lived in the area. But whoever he or she was, they had spotted her and moved in like she was prey.

The werewolf moved closer, crunching meadow grass under his paws as he approached. And she noticed quickly enough that he was male. His cock was huge. The damn beast was built like a horse. She didn't need to be a genius to know that in their fur they were not compatible, at least she didn't think they were.

Instinct told her to run. Curiosity made her hesitate. This creature, twice her size, approached through the grass and neared. She could smell his strength, his confidence, and his domination. In her beast form, the overwhelming urge to belly-up consumed her, to submit to his power, and surrender to a cock that would surely rip her in two.

Silver eyes glowed at her through the darkness as he drew nearer, his massive head and wide jowls appearing in more detail. Teeth longer than her fingers glistened white in the moonlight. His mouth parted, and a long tongue hung over his lower row of teeth.

This brute knew they couldn't mate. That cock between his hind legs would tear her in two if he tried to enter her. And it seemed to grow in size as he stalked closer.

What do you want, wolf-man? She lowered her head and growled at him.

He raised his head, and his ears went forward, as if he couldn't believe she would take such a tone with him. Well if he thought he could scare her into submitting with his size and presence, he had another thing coming. Lust might make her submit, but not fear.

His low growl sent shivers racing through her. Instead of continuing to walk toward her, he began moving around her, and she darted to the side to keep him in front of her.

You are not mounting this bitch tonight, she growled, *not with a cock that size.*

He moved faster than lightning. She wasn't prepared for his sudden attack, an act of pure aggression. The huge beast charged toward her, ripping ground and sending dirt flying.

She howled. *What the fuck?* Her reaction wasn't quick enough. He pounced on her, grabbing her by the nape of the neck.

Oh, my God! He would kill her. But what had she done? Her mind raced as instinct and emotion bombarded each other. She could feel those long, thick teeth press into her skin on the back of her neck. If she twisted they would tear through her flesh.

Her thoughts wouldn't focus. With little effort, it seemed, her paws left the ground. She opened her mouth to scream, and her skin pulled against his teeth. A helpless yelp escaped her throat as she watched the ground beneath her.

Before she could make sense of this brute's action, he released her, and she hit the ground, falling to the side before she could regain her footing.

What the hell did you do that for? She could have slapped herself for getting mouthy when she focused on those massive teeth.

The massive werewolf grew larger, his front paws moving to the side of his body and lengthening, thick glossy coat shrinking into his skin and human flesh appearing.

My sex god!

She watched his long teeth shrink into his mouth, and the shape of his head change. Silver eyes changed to dark blue, and white fur grew in length and turned blond.

"Change," he said simply, when his mouth had the ability to form words.

She stared in awe at the gorgeous naked man in front of her. He hadn't completed the change yet, and his chest muscles remained too large for a normal man. Her gaze dropped quickly toward his middle, and her mouth went dry, and then seemed too wet, as she stared at the cock that hung, not quite erect, between his legs.

That thing could still do bodily damage.

She would be willing to take that risk. Her heart pounded so hard that it took a minute of quick breaths to get the blood to stream through her at a level that would allow her to think.

He had told her to change, and she couldn't think of anything she would like more. It was too good to be true that she had run into this image of perfection that stood in front of her. The change rippled through her until she too stood naked in the meadow before him.

"Hello there, wolf-man." She took a step toward him, the cold night air attacking her bare skin, giving her shivers, and hardening her nipples into painful nubs. "Will you keep me warm?"

"You will walk." And he began changing in front of her, his body once again transforming, until his hands were again paws and he dropped to all fours.

"What the hell?" She glared at him. "It's freezing out here and you think I'm going to walk in my skin?"

As Cariboo *lunewulf* he stood as tall as she did, and at five feet, six inches, she had never considered herself short.

But now she stared into silver eyes with a jaw large enough to snap her neck. She didn't fear him, but he confused her, and she had no intention of letting him know the latter.

He pulled his fur-covered lips back, and revealed long white teeth to her. His growl told her to get moving, and if that wasn't enough incentive, he stepped into her, lowering his head so that his massive skull pushed into her breasts. The hardness of his head, covered by thick white fur as coarse as raw silk, stroked her skin, and raptured her senses.

"Hey. I get the idea." She tripped over the uneven ground.

She stumbled to her knees, the rough ground rubbing her skin raw, and went down on all fours.

His long, hard nose pushed into her rear end, and for a moment she thought he was trying to mount her in his fur. She rolled over to her side, the sensation of him touching her exposed ass raising her body temperature, although the cold night air attacked her senses too, leaving her hot and cold at the same time.

Meadow grass prickled her backside as she sat on her rear and stared up into his open mouth with fangs hanging past his lower jaw, and a large red tongue hanging out between them. A monster of dreams breathed into her face, silver eyes glowing in the night, and white fur making his massive head appear almost to glow surrounded by the darkness.

"What do you want from me?" She didn't understand his strange behavior.

His gaze lowered to her chest. She looked down too, and noticed her rapid breathing by the rise and fall of her breasts.

His tongue swiped over one breast, the rough heat raking over her skin. It had been a while since she had enjoyed a man in his fur while she was in her skin, and she had forgotten how hot it was like this. She watched him as he took a step backwards, and lowered his head to nudge between her legs.

"Oh shit." His hard, damp nose pressed against her shaven pussy.

She fell back on to her elbows, watching as this massive werewolf inspected her.

His long teeth pressed against her tender skin, threatening to puncture her. The thought that he could tear into her with those dagger-like teeth chilled her with nervous anticipation. Yet his touch made her swell with desire, made her soaked, and filled the cold air around them with the scent of lust.

There was no pleasure in pain, although she never shied away from rough sex.

His eyes fluttered shut, apparently instinct reacting to her rich, sweet scent. Her sex god stroked her throbbing pussy with his tongue, a long, slow torturous path, beginning low, at her rear end, and licking her up to her clit. He explored her with his tongue. Thick and wide, hot and wet, and pliable — she had never experienced anything like it. He slipped his tongue inside her, absorbing her cum, and its roughness sent her over the edge.

He pulled his tongue out, and then thrust it inside her further, fucking her in a way no human could. Her eyes rolled back in her head as she felt the pressure of an orgasm build within her, her muscles tightening in anticipation.

"Oh yes. God." She let her head drop back and spread her legs further so that she could allow the beast's large head room between her legs.

His coarse hair brushed against her inner thighs, his moist nose pushed against her throbbing clit, and teeth sharper than knives threatened to tear skin so tender it left her on edge, wanting to give herself over completely to his manipulations, but unable to let go of how dangerous this act could be. In spite of that fact, his actions made her more excited than anything any man had ever done to her before.

She could feel it coming, rippling through her like a growing tidal wave, an orgasm like she had never experienced before. A howl tore from her throat as she reached for him, her body convulsing from his torturous manipulations.

Cold air rushed over her soaked pussy, and she raised her head, confused in her current state of lust, the aftershocks still rippling through her while cum soaked her pussy.

"Please don't stop," she begged, staring up at the werewolf who watched her, slowly licking his lips with that incredible tongue as he backed away from her.

He growled, a low rumble coming deep from his chest. Then without another word, he turned and began walking slowly across the meadow.

"Hey." She scrambled to her feet, her legs not wanting to cooperate, feeling like jelly. "Where are you going?"

Even though he walked, with his size, his stride allowed him to move rather quickly across the field. It was a struggle to keep up with him, and prickly meadow grass made the task a chore in her bare feet. Not to mention she was freezing in the night air.

"This is ridiculous," she mumbled, and allowed the change to ripple through her.

Her bones popped and stretched, and muscles grew within her as she dropped to all fours. Her senses alerted, growing in their awareness to her surroundings, and the black of the night paled around her when her eyes changed to silver.

She dropped to all fours, and then tensed when her giant werewolf turned on her. *I'm not going to freeze to death out here.* She allowed her growl to rumble through her throat, not baring her teeth. The man was twice her size and weight, and with his unpredictable behavior, she didn't want to upset him.

His bark was quick and demanding, and then he turned and broke into a run. She ran after him, guessing that was what he wanted her to do.

When they entered a wooded area, thick with tall pines, and a bed of needles beneath them, he slowed to a walk, nudging her every minute or so as if directing her. The sweet smell of the trees made it hard to smell anything else, and she was surprised for a minute when they entered a clearing and she spotted a large ranch house, situated on a hill, with the pines surrounding it.

Are you taking me to your den, wolf-man?

He stopped in front of barn doors, the largest of the outbuildings near the ranch, and transformed in front of her, this time all of the way.

"I'm glad to see you have some sense of obedience about you," he said, and she was disappointed to see him reach for a pair of jeans.

She changed too, and then stood naked before him, wrapping her arms around her chest in an attempt to keep warm.

"What's that supposed to mean?" She watched him pull his jeans up over his muscular legs, and wanted to pout when that well-endowed cock disappeared as he buttoned his fly.

"I doubt our pack leader approved your run this evening." He grabbed the handle to the barn door, and pulled, shoulder and back muscles rippling under well-tanned flesh as he slid the large door to the side. "And if he did, surely he didn't know of your intent to run alone."

She almost ducked when he turned and grabbed her, his large fingers wrapping around her naked shoulder, and guided her roughly into the large barn. Warmth surrounded her instantly, but she wasn't sure if it was because she was inside the barn, or from the heat of his touch. She could smell the thick scent of horses, but couldn't see in the dark with her human eyes.

He pulled her across a wooden floor, and she watched as he reached for a light switch on a pole. Florescent rods, attached to beams above her, filled the area with light. Horses shuffled in their stalls, not pleased with the rude interruption of their sleep.

She looked up at his expression as he continued to drag her through the barn, and over toward a long table built out from the wall. His beard, trimmed close to his face, and blond curls that fell over his forehead, distracted her from seeing his expression.

"You didn't seem to mind too much that I was out on my own when we were in the meadow," she reminded him, her pussy still aching for more of his attention.

"I wanted to make sure you hadn't just been fucked," he informed her, and then released her to open the top drawer of a dresser along the edge of the table. He pulled out a plaid blanket and shook it out. "This should keep you warm."

"Well I hadn't." She ignored the blanket, and tried to walk into his arms. "But if you would like to finish what you started."

He grabbed her hair, and thrust the blanket at her. She stumbled backwards as he pulled her head back so that she looked up at him.

"My little woman..." he began.

"My name is Simone." She held the blanket with one hand, and grabbed his wrist, although she couldn't get her fingers around it.

"Simone."

She liked the way he said her name, his voice raspy as he accented each syllable.

"If you wish to act like a tramp around me when we are alone, that is fine. I will enjoy it." He pulled her hair harder, and lowered his face toward hers. His sapphire colored eyes sparkled with emotion, but she couldn't tell if he was angry, or turned on. "But if I catch you acting like this around any other wolf, he shall die, and you will get some sense beat into you. Is that clear?"

Normally she would have kneed any man in the groin who dared to speak to her like that. No one ran her life, and she didn't care much for threats. But for some reason that she couldn't identify, she didn't want to fight him. She nodded her head the best that she could.

"What's your name?" she whispered, wishing more than anything that he would kiss her.

The sound of a truck pulling up outside caught both their attention. Simone heard a door slam shut, and footsteps, then muffled voices.

"My name is Rock." He let her go, turning his attention toward the barn door, then walked away from her, his back muscles moving with his confident stride.

He disappeared, shutting the barn door behind him, and Simone wrapped the blanket around her. She hurried over to the door, and had to allow part of the change to increase the size of her muscles so that she could pull the large wooden door to the side, and see what was going on outside.

"Oh shit." She noticed the pale blue Suburban, and a moment later realized Johann stood talking to a man she didn't recognize.

Rock walked toward the two men, but apparently the sound of her opening the barn door triggered his attention. He turned and stalked back toward her.

She wasn't prepared for him to grab her arm and lift her off the ground.

"Hey! Put me down." She kicked before she realized she was fighting him.

"You will learn to behave," he hissed at her, and almost tossed her into the barn. "You are not clothed, and I will not have you traipsing out there naked in front of other men." He pointed a finger at her. "Now stay."

She didn't know whether to be outraged or flattered. He marched back out of the barn, and slammed the door shut, as if it were no heavier than a screen door.

Her senses returned to her quickly. Johann was out there. And she had no doubts that he had just witnessed this Cariboo *lunewulf* manhandling her.

"Well hell," she muttered, not sure whether she should go back out there and deal with the wrath of Johann, or stay in here, and avoid the wrath of her sex god.

Chapter Five

Rock Toubec closed the barn door, and turned to face his ranch manager and the new pack leader. Neither one of them looked too pleased, and he could only guess what their conversation might have been up to this point.

"Sir, we got our new pack leader here asking to see you." Martin Hanson turned on his good leg, and then limped a step or two, as he approached. The old injury he'd sustained in a pack fight didn't slow him in his duties; the man was always on top of things. "He says he has a couple questions," Hanson added under his breath.

"I assume you're Rock Toubec." A *lunewulf* approached him, hand extended, and he appraised the guarded expression on the man's face. The man's eyes pierced right through him, summing him up. "I'm Johann Rousseau. I don't believe we've met yet."

He watched as Rousseau looked over his shoulder and nodded toward the barn.

"You've got Simone Rousseau in there," Johann said, and started walking toward the barn.

Hanson hurried after the pack leader, but Rock gestured for him to hold off. "Is she your bitch?" he asked Rousseau.

Rock watched the man turn around and meet his gaze. He didn't smell fear, or hostility; the man simply stared at him.

Rousseau sighed and rubbed his face, taking a step or two toward Rock. The darkness around them shadowed his expression, but Rock kept a careful eye on the man's gaze. Rousseau never looked away from him.

"Simone is a single bitch, out without an escort." Rousseau kept his tone calm and relaxed, and his scent unreadable, but Rock thought he heard a hard edge in the man's voice. "I'm taking her home."

"To your place." Reciting pack law didn't impress him.

"Yes." Rousseau turned and walked toward the barn door again.

"So she is your slut." Rock watched the muscles tighten through the back of Rousseau's shirt when he stopped in his pace at the comment.

"She's going to get that reputation if I leave her locked up in your barn." Rousseau turned to face him, and Rock realized the man would fight over the matter.

"Are you planning on hauling her off my land every time I get her out here?" Rock felt instincts surge through him, and the desire to protect what was on his property urged him to change.

"Do you wish her for a mate?" Rousseau put his hands on his hips and narrowed his brow.

He wouldn't be cornered into any shotgun mating. "I haven't had a chance to get to know the bitch yet."

A cold wind slapped at his bare chest and back. He could feel the hairs move on his skin, and wondered what his naked bitch was doing in his barn. It actually surprised him that she remained in there. Maybe she feared her pack leader more than she did him. He didn't like that idea.

More than likely, she stayed in there because of his last command.

"You're more than welcome to come call on her sometime." Rousseau turned again toward the barn, this time his stride more determined. "It would do her good to have some official dates instead of romps in the meadows when she is out by herself."

The man spoke loud enough for the bitch in his barn to hear him. She had said her name was Simone. And he could see already she was wild enough to have defied any order this pansy of a pack leader had to give. Not to mention, she liked to fuck.

"She won't be fucking strangers anymore." He decided to let the *lunewulf* open the barn door by himself, relishing the fact that the wolf would have to put on some muscle to do it.

Rousseau slid open the barn door, and he had to give the pack leader credit for not balking under the heaviness of the steel-lined door. In the next second however, a white flash darted free of her confinement, and he realized his little bitch was hell-bent on escape.

"What the fuck?" Rousseau yelled, and turned as Simone flew past him.

Rock allowed the beast within him to surface, and encouraged the change, forcing blood to pump through his veins faster than a human could tolerate, feeling the bones stretch through his body, as the creature within him took its form.

Little bitch, you will learn to behave! He snarled, and leapt into the air feeling the impact of her smaller body collide with his. Simone went flying, tumbling head over paws as she rolled along the ground. He took advantage of the moment where she lay stunned on the ground and pounced on her, grabbing her by the nape of the neck.

"Toubec. You can't handle her like that!" Rousseau yelled at him, his voice garbled.

He tossed Simone toward the Suburban and changed just enough to talk to her. If she tried to run, he would capture her easily enough.

"Get in the truck, bitch. I will deal with you tomorrow." He hovered over her, and could smell Rousseau come up behind him.

He watched the pack leader open the back door of the SUV and give Simone a nudge in the rear with his foot. She jumped into the truck, not changing, and kept her back to both of them as she lay down on the seat.

Stubborn little thing. He liked her more and more every minute.

* * * * *

Simone rolled over in her bed, sore muscles singing to life along with memories of the night before. Jere sat on the floor, playing with her dolls.

Who was this Cariboo *lunewulf* who had sent her over the edge with the best orgasm she had experienced in ages, and at the same time bullied her unlike any wolf she had ever known? Heat spread inside her, her insides swelling with desire that made it hard to lie still. She wanted to stretch out under her covers, and run her hands over her breasts, pinching her nipples, and feed the craving that surged through her with violent tendencies.

Her pussy swelled, her rich cream soaking her pussy lips, and her fingers begged to slide over her firm tummy, down to soothe the growing humidity between her legs.

She wanted to rub that ache away, even though she knew if she stroked herself, fucked her pussy with her fingers, it wouldn't be enough.

Thoughts of that massive cock, and how it might feel inside her, made her pussy pulsate with need. She tightened her thigh muscles and felt cum soak her pussy lips. She wanted to bury herself under the covers, fuck her cunt with her fingers, and drown in the rich scent of her lust.

No. That wasn't true. What she wanted was to straddle Rock Toubec, and slide her soaked pussy on to that huge cock. She wanted to feel him inside her, impaling her. She wanted to ride that cock until she screamed.

Her daughter dressed one of her dolls. Jere talked quietly to herself, entranced in her own little world. The best thing to do would be to spend the day with her daughter, look for work, get Jere enrolled in school, and keep her mind off of Rock Toubec, and that massive cock of his.

All she knew about him was that he was Cariboo *lunewulf*, and his name was Rock. She knew more than that, though. He was powerful, demanding, a predator not to be reckoned with. He had threatened her, overpowered her, and issued orders that normally she would ignore. But there was something about him, something raw and untamed, carnal and dangerous.

And he said he would deal with me today.

"Mommy. You're awake." Jere had turned to look at her, and now smiled her daddy's smile, dropping her dolls to crawl into bed. "Get up, Mommy."

She took her time before heading to the kitchen for that first cup of coffee she was dying to have. There would be no pleasure facing Johann and hearing his cutting remarks about the night before. And she sure didn't want to hear any lectures.

"I hear you had a rough night last night." Samantha put a stack of dishes in the cabinet, then turned to give her friend an assessing look.

"Who is out there?" She gestured toward the living room, where Johann sat with two men that she didn't recognize.

She walked over to pour coffee, and then sipped at the wonderful rich brew. She felt her insides liven with appreciation and took another sip.

"Several men here to complain about the mating law." Samantha lowered her voice, and leaned against the counter. "I guess they aren't happy having to share one bitch."

"Can't say that I blame them." But it was a good thing that Johann was tied up, and she didn't have to listen to him bitch at her about the night before.

"He wants to talk to you though."

"I don't want to talk to him." She glanced toward the living room. "Maybe Jere and I can slip out of here while he is still busy."

"We did discuss you and me running some errands today." Samantha shot a worried look toward the living room. "But he would be pissed if we left without saying anything."

"I have things I need to do."

His actions weren't justified, and he needed to learn she wouldn't be at his beck and call just because Jere was his daughter.

Maybe she had run to him every time he wanted to fuck when they were younger, but that was then. Things were different now, and she was not his slut. As far as she could see, Johann owed her an apology for his intrusion last night. Hell, she might have known her Cariboo *lunewulf* a lot better if Johann hadn't sniffed his way into the picture.

The phone rang, and she reached for it, making eye contact with Johann, who leaned against the wall in the living room. His dark blue eyes penetrated through her, triggering her defenses, and she turned away before she snarled at him. That would only make matters worse.

"Hello." She cradled the phone, and went to get cereal for her daughter.

Jere took the hint, and climbed into one of the chairs at the table.

"I need to speak with Johann Rousseau," a baritone drawled.

"He's busy right now." Simone grabbed milk and put it on the table. She sat down and poured cereal into two bowls.

"Is this his queen bitch?" The male voice seemed to purr into her ear.

Simone watched Samantha ease into the chair next to her, holding the round bulge of her tummy with her hand. Her friend seemed to glow this morning.

"No. Did you want to talk to her?"

"Simone." The way he said her name sent chills racing over her skin.

She held her spoon in midair when she realized who the caller was.

Rock.

Her mouth went dry, while heat raced through her body, pooling between her legs, cum soaking her inner thighs. Just the man's voice over the phone sent her senses into overdrive. She fumbled for coherency, trying to get her mind to work, and to think of something to say. Images of his naked body teased her ruthlessly, making rational thought impossible.

"This is Simone." Her voice cracked, and Samantha looked her way, an eyebrow rising.

Her emotions saturated the air around them. Jere looked at her confused, not understanding the barrage of scents her mother released. And Samantha had a look of concern, maybe even worry. She didn't like either of their reactions. No man ever controlled her with the simple use of her name. What was wrong with her?

"What are you doing today?" His words curled around her, teasing her with the roughness of his deep tone.

She opened her mouth to tell him she had errands, of her plans to look for work, and to enroll Jere in a preschool. But what would be the purpose in all of that? He didn't care about her daily itinerary. And she sure didn't answer to him. Granted, she wanted to sample what he had to offer. And if she played her cards right, it seemed likely he would fuck her. But he didn't own her, and she wouldn't fall for a man who would control and bully her.

When are you ever going to learn? She took a deep breath and forced her emotions under control. He was just another werewolf. Regardless of his size, he would use her and walk away, just like all the others. She needed to learn to take charge of the using. That way her feelings would not be involved, and she wouldn't get hurt.

"I haven't decided what I'm going to do today," she said, relaxing and feeling a bit of control return to her overheated senses. "And who is this calling?"

"This is Rock Toubec." He paused, while she repeated his name in her head. Rock Toubec. She liked the sound of it. Hard, just like he was. "Do you have so many men calling you that you can't identify them?"

Simone chuckled, forcing her cheer into the conversation, even though her heart pounded in her chest.

"Well now, darling. I've only been in town a few days. Give me a chance. Not that many people know that I am here yet."

"Good." Calm satisfaction rang through in his response. "I will be busy most of the day, so I won't be able to get to you until after supper. What time is good for you?"

"Anytime, I guess." Her heart beat in her chest with painful explosions. He was asking her out. She would get to see him today!

Her pussy throbbed in nervous anticipation. Blood pumped through her veins, making her cunt throb in rhythm to her heartbeat. She would ride that cock tonight, she would see to it. Cum rushed through her at the thought, making her almost dizzy as waves of raw lust consumed her.

"I will be there as soon as it is dark."

He didn't say goodbye. An emptiness that she didn't quite understand filled her when she heard the click in her ear as the line went dead. She stood slowly to put the phone on the receiver. It took her a minute to realize everyone in the room watched her, including Johann.

She met his displeased look when she looked up to place the cordless on the wall cradle.

"Who was that?" He crossed his arms and leaned in the doorway, staring down at her with an expression that bordered on outrage.

He would not intimidate her, and she no longer gave a rat's ass what he thought. She had a date. This wasn't meeting up with a group at the bar and fucking someone out back after hours. This was a prearranged date. And no one, not even Johann, would fuck this up for her.

"That was Rock Toubec." Simone grabbed her cereal bowl, the cereal now soggy, and walked over to the sink to dump it, doing her best to ignore the spicy smell of anger that filled the room.

"I want to talk to you outside." Johann took her arm as he moved into the kitchen, and started toward the back door.

"No." She tried to wrench free of him, but his fingers tightened around her arm, pinching off the circulation. Even if she allowed her muscles to grow, she was no match for him.

"It's okay." Samantha sounded reassuring, and she stared at her, bewildered, wondering why her friend would think it would be okay to be alone with Johann when he was obviously so outraged. "He has something he needs to tell you. Go on. I'll stay in here with Jere."

Chapter Six

Rock leaned against his desk, and watched his fax machine. He never would have guessed that ranching involved so much time inside. The Rousseau ranch, now the Toubec ranch, was a gold mine. He had been at the right place at the right time to snag it for such a deal. But there was a lot he didn't know, and a lot that he had to rely on his hired help to handle for him. That bothered him. He didn't like others doing his work.

Saw milling was second nature for him. He understood the business, and the ranch would profit in that area under his hand. Hanson, his ranch manager, had good knowledge of cattle. The man was old school, and didn't much care for computer printouts and fancy numbers. But this was the twenty-first century, and a deal could go down over the Internet just as easy as it could with a handshake. Since Hanson wouldn't keep up on the cattle market online, Rock had forced himself to pay attention to that end of the business.

He stared at the monitor on his desk. The ranch once had a retreat on it, a place where werewolves could enjoy privacy, and a good vacation. There were cottages, all isolated, and he knew humans had used it for a dude ranch many years before. But now that part of the property sat, unused, because he hadn't found the time to clean up the area and advertise to bring in guests. It needed to be handled though, if he wanted to make this land work for him with all that it had to offer.

"We're headed out to the south pasture." Martin Hanson stuck his head in through the doorway. "You sure you don't want to ride with us?"

"Love to." He squinted as he looked out the windows, staring at the view of one of the barns and the open spread beyond. "There's too much to do here, though."

Hanson hobbled into the room and leaned on the back of one of the chairs facing him.

"Now you ain't gonna spend your day doing housework, are you?" The disapproval in Hanson's tone couldn't be missed.

He sighed, turning his attention to the old man. "That needs to be done too." Housekeepers didn't seem to like his place. After a year, he hadn't been able to keep a woman in this house longer than a week. "But no. The cleaning will have to wait. I need to do some paperwork."

Several hours later, Rock didn't think he could stand four walls being around him any longer. He had heard his boys roughhousing from room to room while he'd been working, and decided a run might be in order for all three of them.

Although he'd been raised in the mountains, this part of British Columbia, with its lush green prairies and endless blue skies, appealed to him very much. The boys darted through the tall grass, blurs of white fur as they tumbled over each other and growled playfully. He nipped at them to keep them headed in the right direction, and before long they had reached the line of pines that indicated they had reached their destination.

His cubs smelled the water, and without permission darted over to splash through the rocky creek. Rock left them to explore, and trotted toward the six cabins hidden back in this isolated patch of tall pine trees.

A smell he hadn't expected brought him to a stop. He sniffed the air, his ears standing at attention to listen for anything that might explain this invasion of scents.

Flesh. He smelled flesh. Decaying and putrid. The odor grew stronger when he neared the cottages, and he moved into the shadows, instinct prevailing. He reached the cabin that had to be the source of the smell, and glanced around him. He could still hear the cubs splashing, more than likely chasing fish, but other than that he detected no one in the area.

He allowed the change to move through him, his bones contorting, his senses changing from beast to human, until he stood naked in the afternoon sun, surrounded by the wretched smell of death and decay. He turned the door handle on the cottage, and then ducked when hundreds of flies swarmed around him. Sunshine filled the dark room, and he didn't bother to enter. He didn't need to. Laying on the floor of the cabin was a woman, or what was left of her. Naked, beaten, and very much dead.

* * * * *

"What do you make of it?" Rock didn't like inviting strangers out to his place.

Cariboo *lunewulf* kept to themselves. But he was a man of ritual. He followed the law, kept to a routine, and found that made life a lot simpler. A naked, dead human lay on his property. He didn't care to deal with humans, but her kin had a right to know. Death was a ritual, a passing over. Even untimely and ugly death had a right to the ceremony of burial.

"My guess is that she has been out here at least a week." Matthew Jordeaux, one of the pack doctors, walked out of the cabin.

He didn't make his comment to Rock, but instead focused on Johann Rousseau. The pack leader still stood inside the cabin, walking around slowly, squinting against the sun.

"How long have you known she was here?" Johann glanced his way briefly, but then looked away, taking in his surroundings.

"Maybe an hour." Rock followed the pack leader's gaze as he looked at the other cabins. "I didn't have a phone on me, so went back to the house to call you."

Rock had hoped his hot little bitch would have answered the phone when he called the pack leader's house, but Johann had answered. He wanted to know where she was, but had dealt with the matter on hand. Thoughts of her distracted him though. Even though this female was human, this was the sort of thing that happened to bitches without escorts. His first wife had died like this, and he knew someone as hot as Simone would suffer a similar fate if she wasn't protected. It was the way of the world.

"Do you know her?" Johann looked back toward the cabin. "Or I should say, did you know her?"

"I don't play with humans." Rock stared at the pack leader, and could tell the man tried to weigh something in his mind. The stench of the human was too strong to detect emotions. "I can have some of my men haul a truck out here and pick her up. What should we do with her?"

"She's human. We've got to let her kind deal with this." Johann started the walk back toward the house.

"I want this place as a retreat." Rock took long strides, frustration building in him. Humans would hamper this isolated sanctuary, and prolong his fixing the cabins to prepare them for visitors. "What we need to do is head into town and figure out who has a missing female."

"The police need to be involved in this, my friend." Johann matched his stride, and Rock had the urge to walk just a bit faster. "You need to be the one to call them, too. Since she is on your land, they will want to question you."

Rock didn't like this, not at all. He wanted the female out of his cabin, and to be done with it. They could tend to her burial once they took her away, but she wasn't his concern, and he didn't want to be dragged into it.

"I'll give them a call," he muttered. And thought while he was at it, he would call the pack leader's house, since he knew Johann wasn't there, and see if he could catch Simone at home.

* * * * *

Get off of my land before I run the lot of you out of here. That is what Rock wanted to say. But he stood silently watching as a handful of Prince George police officers scoured the area, leaving their human smells everywhere. His mood had soured considerably after being questioned by an overweight human female in uniform. He wasn't sure how many different ways she could word the same question. All she seemed to want to know was if he had killed the female. He finally came out and told her he had not.

"We should be out of your hair in no time," she had told him in a friendly tone, although she smelled anything but friendly.

"How could she be out here for five days and you not know she was here?" A burly human wearing a uniform that indicated he had some rank over the others sized him up.

"This is the first I've been over this way in quite a few months." Rock didn't see the point in the question. "If I had known she was out here, I wouldn't have left her lying in there to decay."

"Let the man do his job," Johann muttered next to him.

Rock knew he had to be civil to these humans, or they would be swarming the place. And he knew Rousseau didn't want humans wandering into pack territory any more than he did.

Rock sighed, hating this whole matter. "I reckon this whole thing has me a bit shook up," he told the officer, and could tell the officer wondered whether to believe him.

Well hell. *What am I supposed to say?* He had little experience dealing with humans.

"They are pretty much ready to haul her out of here." The burly human gestured toward the group surrounding the dead female. "If you see anything else out here suspicious, give us a call right away. And we have your number, right?"

Rock nodded, and was more than relieved when they took the dead human away in one of their ambulances.

* * * * *

He still had a couple hours before dark, but his thoughts strayed to his sultry little bitch as he escaped to the musty corner of his barn to check on some repairs that had been done earlier that day.

It kept creeping back into his mind that she hadn't been home when he called over there earlier that day. Or at least he had assumed she wasn't there when Johann had answered, and the house had sounded quiet.

She doesn't answer to you. And he wondered why it was that he wanted her to. He wanted to know where she had been, who she had been with, and what she had been doing. In the year he had lived here, none of the women he had been with had affected him like Simone Rousseau.

And you haven't even fucked her yet. But to mate with a bitch meant that she was yours for life. It was an old pack tradition, honored by few these days. And he knew he had pounded a bitch or two in the meadows with no intention of seeing them again. It had been consenting sex, just the need to get his dick wet. But he was from the old school at heart, and had waited when he took his first mate, because he had known he wanted her to birth his cubs.

Rock stared at the repairs without seeing them, and scowled. He didn't like the direction his thoughts were going. He had no desire to be pure and righteous with Simone Rousseau. He wanted to fuck the shit out of her, and soon. Memories of her naked in the field grass, spread out before him, with the scent of her cum intoxicating him, made it hard for him to concentrate on anything around him.

He stormed out of the house, and decided the only way he would be able to get another thing done before dark was to call her. He would let her know that it was her fault that his cock was rock-hard, and making it impossible to get a damn thing done.

"Hello." The soft female voice that answered the phone raised his blood pressure a fraction. Already he knew that voice.

"Where were you today?" he asked her, closing his bedroom door and walking over to his bed.

"And who is this?" Her teasing tone made his blood boil, his cock growing inside his jeans, pressing for freedom against the restraint of his jeans.

He couldn't stand the pain any longer and yanked at the zipper on his jeans. "I have a feeling you know exactly who this is."

"Now my dear, you forget I grew up here. Many werewolves in this pack know me." She chuckled, and he could hear the blood racing through his brain. "And I'm sure at least a few of them wouldn't mind knowing me again."

Rock closed his eyes, the thought of her out in the town, with some wolf sniffing around her, settled in his stomach with an acidy taste. He had never known such an untamed little bitch. This one was close to out of control, and he was overwhelmed with the desire to be the one to tame her.

"This is Rock, and you damn well know it," he growled, while kicking his jeans off.

He sprawled out on his bed, stretching his long legs, and staring down at his erect cock, a weapon ready to put some manners into a little foxy bitch.

Her laughter seemed softer, as if she realized he had limits that wouldn't be crossed. Good.

"Why Rock, how are you darlin'?" Her voice grew even softer, a sultry sound that made his cock throb as blood pumped through him at a maddening rate.

"Are you going to answer my question?" He adjusted the phone between his shoulder and ear, then grabbed his cock, his entire body stiffening when he pulled on it.

"Well, I spent the day settling in to the town." Her voice was rich and sweet, like honey. He closed his eyes, stroking his cock while listening to her voice. "I put my daughter in preschool so now my days are free."

The thought of her with a lot of free time didn't set well with him. He opened his eyes, his cock pounding in his hand, burning with an angry fire that made it hard to concentrate.

"We will have to find something to keep your days busy then." He had to think to speak, the boiling fury of lust, pent-up longer than he cared to think about, surfaced with newborn energy.

"Oh? And how do you propose to keep me busy?" She teased him. He could see that flirty grin on her face.

You don't really want me to answer that question, my little bitch.

He chuckled, and heard her breathe into the phone. Was she masturbating too? He had so much to learn about her. This woman who was too full of life, with too much energy, and way too beautiful for her own good.

"Tell me what you are doing right now." He started stroking his cock, heat radiating from his shaft.

"I just got out of the shower." She paused for a minute, as if allowing him time to imagine her naked body with droplets of water strolling over tempting curves. "And now I'm standing in my room naked, trying to decide what to wear tonight."

Fire erupted in him, and he tightened his grip on his cock, fighting for control, before he erupted all over himself. Anger and appreciation raced through him at the same time. No bitch controlled his desires. And with a mere phone call, Simone seemed able to put him over the edge.

He forced himself to a sitting position, throwing his legs over the edge of the bed, enduring the pain of his steel-hard cock. He should fuck her and enjoy the ride. Shove his massive cock deep inside her, enjoy her screams of passion, and use her the way he felt sure she had been used before.

This one is worth taming. He heard the small amount of rational thought his brain was able to muster.

"Wear something nice. I will take you to dinner tonight." He would not allow her to force him into fucking the shit out of her within minutes of being alone with her. "I will pick you up in an hour."

"I can't wait," she whispered into the phone.

Rock couldn't wait either. He stood staring out at the sunset long after he hung up the phone with her. Something about this bitch seemed different than other bitches he had met in this pack. She was wild, and no doubt had created a tarnished reputation for herself, if the way she talked to him was any indication of how she talked to other men. But he sensed something, and he couldn't place his finger on it. She would require discipline, and lots of it. He smiled and decided masturbating in the shower before seeing her would be a good idea. He needed to be somewhat coherent when he began training his little bitch to behave.

Chapter Seven

"What are you doing?" Samantha tapped on Simone's bedroom door, and then pushed it open slightly.

Simone turned around, still naked, and smiled, her mood lifted for the first time that day.

"Well at least you aren't scowling anymore." Samantha shut the door behind her, and sat on the bed.

"I'm trying to decide what to wear tonight." She hadn't had time yet to unpack all her clothes, and so dug through the box on the floor. "Something sexy enough to drive him wild."

"You aren't still going to go out with Rock Toubec, are you?" Samantha crossed her legs, and then leaned back on her hands. "Johann will be pissed."

"Well, Johann doesn't have to go." She pulled a black knit sweater from the box, and put it on. "I just got off the phone with Rock, and he is taking me to dinner."

Simone found the black skirt she wanted to wear, and slid into it then zipped it up the side. She turned to face Samantha, posing for her, and watched her friend chew her lip. Her friend would side with her mate; Simone realized that. Johann had no right telling her she couldn't see the wolf simply because he had a wild side to him though.

"What if he killed that human out on his land?" Samantha's expression was full of worry.

Now this murdered human simply added to Samantha's worries. Simone wished she could assure her friend that she didn't detect that kind of hostility in Rock. Call it her primal instincts, but Simone knew the man wouldn't be that cruel.

"He doesn't strike me as the kind of wolf who would go for humans."

Simone waved her off, and opened her closet door to find her boots.

"And Johann's lecturing me about how Rock is too rough on bitches isn't going to make me sit home and twiddle my thumbs." She dragged her boots out, and then plopped on the bed next to Samantha. "This pack is full of a bunch of uptight old biddies. Those men came over the other night to talk to Johann about Rock simply because they like to start trouble."

"That could be true." Samantha snickered, but her worried expression remained. "You and me can handle ourselves," she said quietly. "I know you've had your scrapes, and so have I. But what if something isn't right about him?"

Simone remembered his behavior in the meadow, and thought of the things Johann had mentioned to her earlier that morning. He had told her Rock Toubec had a reputation for being too rough with bitches. And now a dead human was found on his property.

She shrugged her morbid thoughts away. "You must not have gotten a good look at him at the funeral. You wait until you see him up close, and then tell me what you think is not right about him." An image of Rock Toubec, naked, entered her thoughts.

I can't wait to ride that cock. She shivered at the thought, the heat racing through her body with anticipation.

"He's that hot, huh?" Samantha seemed to detect her enthusiasm. "Well I look forward to meeting him then."

Simone hopped up to grab a pair of thigh-highs, and then lay down on the bed, already feeling the dampness in her pussy, and stuck her legs up in the air so she could pull on the hose. Her boots went on next, and then she swirled in front of her friend.

"What do you think?"

Samantha tapped her index finger against her chin. "Tasteful, yet tempting," she said, after some thought. "I think if you are after some dick tonight, you will definitely get it."

The two women burst into giggles, which brought Jere running down the hallway to see what the fun was all about. Simone scooped her daughter into her arms, and led the way back out to the living room.

* * * * *

The women were back in one of the bedrooms when someone knocked on the door. Johann wasn't sure he could handle one more pack member asking questions about the murdered human, or offering their input on the situation. Obviously there was a leak at the Prince George police station, because the entire pack seemed aware of the situation.

"Toubec." Johann thought Simone would have called and cancelled her date with the wolf, but it appeared she had not.

Maybe the wolf was here on different business.

"I'm here for Simone." Rock Toubec ducked his head as he entered into the small living room, and Johann's worries were confirmed that Simone had defied his instruction. "Any news on the dead human?" he asked, while looking around.

"They found out who she was, and I think spoke with the family." Johann watched the Cariboo *lunewulf* give him his full attention.

He wished he could read the man better, but either the werewolf stuffed his emotions very well, or he just didn't have any. Either way, he detected no indication of worry that something might be revealed to convict him. Most of the pack members he'd spoken to today seemed to think Toubec was guilty. They wanted him run out of town.

"I haven't heard anything yet." He needed better connections with the police department.

"One of my hands lives in Prince George. I could send him to you, if you like. He might be able to sniff information out for you."

Johann hadn't expected Toubec to offer assistance in anyway. He studied the man for a minute, cursing his inability to read others better, a trait a pack leader needed to have.

"If you can spare the man." Johann nodded his consent, and then turned when the women entered the room.

"Hi, Rock." Simone put on that sultry smile of hers, the one Johann knew all too well.

She was on the prowl, entering into full tramp mode, and he wanted to forbid her to go out, at least until he could be sure this werewolf was safe.

"Where are you two going?" Johann ignored the glare Simone gave him, and turned his attention to Rock.

The werewolf's expression had changed too. He pulled his gaze from Simone, and Johann studied him, frustrated that he couldn't smell any emotion on the man.

"Johann, I'm not a teenager." Simone chuckled, and walked over to cuddle into Toubec. She slipped her arm around the wolf's massive biceps, and almost appeared dwarfed next to him. "You don't need to wait up for me."

He wanted to bitch-slap her for being so damned bullheaded. This wolf could be a murderer, and she seemed indifferent to that knowledge. Johann opened his mouth to inform Simone she was lucky he was letting her go out at all, when Toubec spoke up.

"Simone." Toubec spoke her name so quietly, Johann almost didn't hear it. "Your pack leader has a right to know your whereabouts."

Johann watched Toubec adjust Simone so that she stood in front of him, with the wolf's hands pressed into her shoulders. Johann wanted to grin at the humbled look the bitch got on her face. He watched her glance over at Samantha, but Johann kept his gaze riveted on Toubec.

"I'm going to take her into town to eat, and we shouldn't be gone more than a few hours," Toubec told him.

Johann nodded and watched the two of them leave his house. He silently willed the wolf to be innocent, because he wasn't sure he had ever seen anyone put Simone in her place so nicely before.

* * * * *

Simone didn't know what to think, and she sure as hell didn't know how to act. Rock took her into Prince George, and wined and dined her with a wonderful steak dinner. He opened her car door, ordered for her, and treated her like a lady.

And why shouldn't someone treat you like a lady?

She didn't know whether to be angry, or flattered. Special treatment like this was foreign to her, and it felt good...damned good. But at the same time, she felt out of her element, on guard, as if suddenly someone would drop the punch line, and the joke would be on her.

She bit down her uneasiness, hating how nervous he made her feel, and tossed her cloth napkin over the remnants of her steak.

What is it about you, Rock Toubec?

Simone decided the rumors about Rock were wrong. Cariboo *lunewulf* may be known for their wild side, but Rock seemed to demand respect wherever he turned. He carried himself with an authority that couldn't be missed, even among the humans. People hurried to help them, made sure they had the best table, continually checked to see that he was happy. Humans were a strange lot, but either Rock Toubec had a known reputation in Prince George, or the people were terrified of him. Either way, she enjoyed the special treatment, and the feeling of warm security she felt when near him.

"So, what now, big guy?" she asked.

She looked up into those turquoise eyes, blue eyes that changed shades so readily with his emotions, and tried a coy grin when he didn't answer right away. His gaze seemed to penetrate right through her, and she felt heat rush through her, gripping her so that she couldn't breathe. The candlelight from the candle in the middle of the table danced unaware, accentuating the strong line of his cheekbone. She took a slow breath, and forced herself to relax, leaning back in her chair and meeting his stare.

"Why are you looking at me like that?" she whispered.

Rock leaned back in his chair as well, stretching his long legs under the table so that one was on either side of hers. She felt his jeans brush against her thigh-highs, and her breath suddenly came in quick pants. He was so big, so long, so powerful looking, and his gaze dark and penetrating. He consumed her space, the air around her soaked with his scent.

"I'm deciding the best way to tame you," he told her, and cocked his head to the side, examining her. Blond waves accented his face, and streaks of pale red highlighted his close shaven beard.

"To tame me?" She laughed, and leaned forward, placing her elbows on the table and giving him what she knew was a damned good shot of cleavage.

His eyes dropped to her tits, but his expression remained serious, his gaze charged with so much heat she could feel it penetrate through her skin.

"You are wild, my little bitch." He spoke barely above a whisper, his deep voice stroking her like thousands of fingers tracing patterns over her skin, giving her chills, and making her feel flushed all at the same time. "I can feel your lustful energy whenever I am around you."

That is because I want you to fuck me, wolf-man.

"Maybe it's your own lustful energy you are feeling." She wouldn't be intimidated by his claim that he would tame her. She had no idea what he meant by that, but no wolf would put a leash on her.

Those turquoise eyes seemed to glow in the dim lighting of the restaurant. Sounds around them faded, and her entire world became him. He stared at her, and she would be damned if she would drop her gaze.

Heat soared through her body, her pussy pulsating furiously along with her heart. No man ever seemed so dominating, so powerful, and so able to bring her to her knees.

"Will you spread your legs for me tonight?" he asked, the vibrancy in his husky whisper about making her explode.

She almost grinned and said that he better fuck her tonight, but then suddenly wondered if he tricked her with his question. He had just accused her of being wild, and needing to be tamed. She had no desire to change her ways, but sensed he would enjoy the challenge if he thought he could..

"Is that what you expect out of this evening?" she asked.

Rock dropped his arm so that his fingers almost touched her elbow, and she thought she saw a small grin appear on his face.

"My expectations have already been fulfilled." He let his gaze travel down her slowly. "You answer me with your question in an attempt to show that you are not eager to fuck. You don't wish me to see you as a wild woman."

Simone ran her fingernail along Rock's arm. Just touching the man turned her insides into molten lava. Her pussy craved his attention so desperately that she could hardly manage to think.

"I wish you to see me for who I am, wolf-man," she whispered, and met his gaze. Fire burned in his eyes, and only added to her already overheated senses. "If you like what you find, then great. If you don't, well, we gave it a shot."

"If I didn't like what I saw, I wouldn't waste my time with you." He looked so damned sexy sitting there, and his words stroked her into a frenzy.

"Then maybe," she whispered. "Maybe the lustful energy belongs to both of us."

She tucked her fingers inside his, and watched the lazy smile play across his face.

"You are playing with fire, little bitch."

She wondered if the fire within him matched the heat that consumed her. Need for him pounded through her, making it difficult to control her senses. He would smell her desire if she weren't careful, and then she would be at his mercy. For some reason, she needed to keep an upper hand with this wolf.

"If I'm such the wild woman that you claim me to be, then you must know I like playing with fire."

He squeezed her hand, the pressure smashing her fingers together and pressing her fingernails into her skin.

"As long as you don't jump from fire to fire, then we will have no problems."

Simone stared at him, momentarily at a loss for words. The intensity of his gaze grew, and he pulled her hand to his mouth.

"Tell me now that you won't go to another wolf."

She could feel his breath singe the hairs on her hand. Her heartbeat raced in her chest, and her mouth seemed to go dry. *Is he really asking me for a commitment?*

"Tell me now, little bitch," he growled, and his demand of her loyalty turned her on more than she ever would have guessed.

She could feel the cum soaking her inner thighs, and his domination gripped her thoughts, consumed her with a desire to do anything he said, anything if he would take care of her growing ache to have him inside her.

"I won't go to another wolf."

Chapter Eight

Rock felt his cock harden with her words. They were only words, and it would be her actions that mattered. But it was a start.

Her scent drifted to his brain as he held her hand, and he couldn't help but taste her before he released her. He took one finger between his teeth and consumed her taste along with her smell like a starved dog.

They needed to leave before he wouldn't be able to move. The throbbing in his cock warned him he would leave that restaurant with a visible hard-on if he didn't get up and start walking soon. "It's time to leave," he told her, releasing her hand, and the warmth of her body at the same time.

She giggled, and he felt for sure she knew the conversation was affecting him.

"You never said what we were doing next." Simone walked next to him, her rich, sexy scent reeking havoc on his libido.

He knew what he wanted to do next. His cock screamed for attention, and he knew Simone would be a willing partner. "We will go have a drink."

Staying in public areas would be best for the evening. He had told himself tonight would be to see what type of bitch Simone Rousseau really was. He liked her wild side, her free spirit, and she was absolutely beautiful. She walked with an air about her that told others around her she wouldn't be intimidated. Her silky blonde hair fell in layers just past her shoulders, just enough to grab onto and hold her in place. The sweater she wore with no bra showed off the firm curve of her breasts, and her large nipples puckered against the cold night air. Or maybe she was as horny as he was.

"What bar were you thinking about going to?" She chewed her lip, and turned to face him when they reached his truck.

"Shall we go where you go with your friends?" He smelled her worry immediately, but didn't know its source.

Simone stepped forward, running her palms up his chest. The heat of her touch sent electricity through his bloodstream, charging him with energy that flowed straight to his cock.

"Wouldn't you rather go somewhere where we could be alone?" She leaned into him, stretching her body against his, those large breasts pressing against his chest.

He grabbed her wrists, needing to prevent her from seducing him right here in the parking lot of one of Prince George's finer restaurants.

"A lesson in etiquette is also in order," he mumbled, and took both of her wrists in one hand so he could open his truck door with the other. "Get in."

She climbed into the cab, and then crawled over to the passenger side, giving him a wonderful ass shot. He narrowed in on the black line of her thong as it disappeared down her ass, and thought his cock would explode right there on the spot.

She adjusted herself in the passenger seat, and turned and smiled. The bitch knew exactly what to do with her body, and exactly how her body affected him.

Pulling his keys out of his pocket took some effort, not to mention the pain he felt climbing into his truck. He needed to get control of himself. After all, he was Cariboo *lunewulf*, the most powerful werewolf ever to stalk the land. And this little *lunewulf* bitch would not get the better of him.

They would go to Howley's, the local werewolf poolroom just off the highway. It didn't take too long to get there, and he recognized a fair amount of the vehicles when they pulled into the large gravel lot.

This time she sat in the passenger seat and waited for him to walk around the truck and open her door. He knew the bitch wasn't stupid. Maybe she would adhere to proper behavior faster than he anticipated. If so, little Simone might prove to be the mate he had been searching for ever since his last mate died. Wild and free-spirited, sexy and intelligent, and with enough sense to know when to behave, and when to be naughty.

"I haven't been here for years." She turned to face him, but her gaze focused on the flat-roofed building surrounded by the darkness of the parking lot.

"You will see old friends." He smelled nervousness on her, and when she turned to look at him, something almost akin to fear marred her pretty blue eyes.

He didn't like uncertainty in this little bitch. He liked her feistiness, the fighter that he saw in her. Whatever it was that suddenly bothered her, he would know its source.

"I don't know about old friends." She turned and stared up at him, her wide eyes changing to a deep shade of blue. "I wasn't exactly the most popular kid on the block."

He watched her inhale, and her sweater spread over those full round mounds of flesh. She scooted to the edge of the seat, her legs pressing against his. He reached out and grabbed her under the armpits, and let his thumbs tease the points in her sweater.

"You are safe with me," he told her, and lifted her to him.

She wrapped her arms around his neck, and grinned. "You'd make one hell of a protector, my big bad wolf."

Howley's parking lot wasn't the same as uptown, where the restaurant had been. And he didn't mind kissing the hell out of her right here. He crushed his mouth over hers, devouring the taste of her, so sweet, and so fucking hot. She met him with an eagerness that didn't surprise him, but he knew if he didn't maintain control, she would have them fucking in the cab of his truck. He doubted the cab would survive the act.

He squeezed her breast, and the groan she made about drove him mad. Her nipple was so hard, so ready for his mouth to nibble on and suck, that he began to doubt his reasoning for taking her into the pool hall.

Because you want to know the bitch before you fuck her silly.

He wanted to tell his sound reasoning to go to hell.

"We're going inside," he ordered, as much to himself as to her.

Her giggle was like a drug seeping through his system.

"You're the boss."

He picked her up and then put her on the ground, shutting the truck door behind her.

"I'm glad to see your training is off to a good start." He grinned at her surprised expression, and then fought off laughter when she turned and smacked him in the chest.

"Don't push your luck, wolf-man."

The usual crowd was out tonight. Some of his ranch hands drank at the bar, and a few wolves from in town shot darts over in the corner. There were some humans in the place as well. It was good policy not to discriminate, and as long as they didn't cause trouble, Rock knew Shackley, the old biker who ran the place, wouldn't kick them out. Most turned and acknowledged his entrance with a nod. He noticed the lingering looks as they took in the hot little bitch on his arm, but none of them would mess with her, or offer any comments. They all knew better.

Shackley placed a couple cold bottles of beer on the counter as they approached and nodded. "Good to see you, Toubec," and then turned his attention to Simone. "I heard you all came back to the pack."

"Did you miss me, Shackley?" Her tone had lowered, soft and thick like honey.

Shackley snorted, and turned away from the two of them.

"Simone?" A bitch approached them, touching Simone on the sleeve. She looked to be about Simone's age, but somewhat worn down. "Is that you?"

Rock watched the two bitches laugh, and give each other hugs. They quickly fell into catch-up chatter, and he leaned on the nearest bar stool, taking a long drink of his beer.

Derek Rousseau, the dead pack leader's oldest son, entered the bar, and walked toward him. Rock didn't like the wolf—never had. He was a backstabber and a cheat—just not as good at it as his grandmother had been. Derek leaned against the bar and waited for Shackley to notice him. Rock took small pleasure in the fact that the old bartender took his time in waiting on the man.

"Hear they're finding dead bodies out at your place." Derek finally snapped his fingers to get Shackley's attention.

Rock didn't feel a need to comment on the obvious.

"Rumor has it you killed the human."

Rock stared at the werewolf, watching him shift from one foot to the other. The stale stench of discomfort radiated from the man, and Rock hoped the wolf would go find someone else to bother.

"Just a rumor, mind you." Derek looked past him at Simone and the other bitch. "Well, well. You out with Johann's piece of ass tonight, are you?"

Simone coughed, catching his attention. He set his bottle of beer on the counter carefully, fighting the urge to slam it against the wooden surface. Thoughts of tossing Derek Rousseau out of the bar on his skinny ass seemed rather appealing at the moment.

"I am no one's piece of ass." Simone jumped in front of him, her beer bottle raised, either ready to pour beer over the lame excuse for a werewolf, or to hit him upside the head with the bottle. Rock wasn't sure which one.

Rock grabbed her arm, pulling her back to his side.

"You got one minute to get your ass out of this bar," he growled at the astonished wolf. "If I have to throw you out, I promise you won't enjoy it."

"You're throwing your power around a bit too much." Derek slammed his unfinished beer down on the counter, and turned to retreat. "I, for one, will celebrate the day the pack boots you out of town."

Derek turned to leave, and nodded to the bitches. "Gertrude, you stay away from her or she will tarnish your reputation."

Rock let go of Simone, and grabbed the wolf by the collar.

"What the fuck?!" The wolf squirmed under the attack, but in skin or fur, the man was no match.

Rock used Derek's body to push open the front door. "I'll kick your fucking ass if you ever talk about her like that again." He tossed Derek toward the parking lot, and turned around without bothering to see if the man fell or not.

"Well hell." Rock watched Simone run toward the back door of the bar. The bitch who had been talking to her looked at him and then turned toward the table where she had been sitting.

Rock pulled his wallet out and tossed a bill on the counter, then hurried after Simone.

"Simone!" he yelled, as soon as the back door to the bar closed behind him.

He used the darkness around him as a cloak, and allowed his bones to shift just enough that his senses heightened.

Every smell around him became more acute, and the black of the night slowly turned to gray.

He walked to the edge of the building and caught sight of her at the other end.

He picked up his pace, reaching the other end of the building in moments. Her boots crunched against the gravel, and he allowed the change to revert him back to human form.

"Don't run away from me."

She stopped walking and crossed her arms over her large breasts.

"I should have refused to go in there." She didn't look at him, but focused on the ground.

"That asshole is a waste of wolf flesh. I promise he won't bother you again."

Her blue eyes burned with fury when she looked up at him.

"Then it will be someone else, Rock." She threw her arms up in exasperation. "Just take me home."

Her hair flew around her shoulders when she turned to walk toward the truck, but he grabbed her arm. She had to see that he wasn't bothered by that jerk's words. Hell. The man had insulted him, too. But he wouldn't waste energy getting angry over a peon's accusations.

"I'll take you home when I'm damned good and ready." He grabbed her other arm, and held her so she faced him. "I want to spend more time with you."

"You don't get it, do you?" she hissed. "Derek was right. I was Johann's slut. I spread my legs for him any time he wanted. Anywhere he wanted. Hell, I fucked him in front of groups of people. I didn't care. I like to fuck. And for some reason this world gives women who like to fuck a bad name."

Her breath came in gasps, heaving her large breasts up and down, cleavage springing forth through the stretched material of her sweater.

"Fucking is a good thing." He grinned at the scowl she gave him. "I don't mind a bit that you enjoy it so much."

She squirmed in his grasp, and then kicked his leg. He let her go, feeling the sharp pinch in his shin from the tip of her boot. He had no desire to discipline her in a public parking lot, not after the abuse she had just taken inside the bar. But he hardened his gaze and lowered his voice.

"Don't do that again, little bitch."

She didn't answer, but turned around and stormed away from him, her adorable ass swishing from side to side in her short miniskirt. And she wasn't headed toward the truck.

He took several long strides, grabbed her arm, and dragged her toward his truck. He almost threw her in the passenger side, and slammed the truck door then headed around the front.

"I'm not going anywhere with you." She pushed her door open again and jumped out. "You are too angry."

He was on her in an instant.

"You haven't seen me angry," he told her. "Now get back in the truck before I tie you down."

"You wouldn't dare."

Her eyes opened wide when he grabbed her arm, and then reached into the back of his truck where a coil of clothes line happened to be. He had meant to redo the clothes line he had behind his house, and now was glad he hadn't gotten to it. He ripped the plastic open with his teeth, and then found the end of the rope.

"What the hell are you doing?" She looked shocked, but the anger in her tone seemed to have disappeared.

He flipped her around, and then pressed her down so that her face pressed into the front seat. Her adorable round ass pressed against his thigh, and the overwhelming urge to fuck her silly right there consumed him. He fought the cloud of lust that filled his brain, and wrapped the white rope around her wrists, then ripped the line with his teeth, threw the excess in the back of his truck, and made a nice knot, pinning her hands together behind her back.

He couldn't help himself when he moved his hands to lift her into the truck. He took a moment to feel her soft ass, nicely exposed with the black thong disappearing down toward her pussy. The black material was soaked.

"I'll have to remember that fighting makes you horny as hell," he whispered, running his fingers over her shaved pussy, and feeling the thick cream soak his fingers. "Damn woman."

"Rock," she whimpered.

He lifted her up, and tossed her on to the seat, in somewhat of a sitting position, then shut her truck door once again. The walk around the front of the truck in the cold night air wasn't enough to calm the fire that burned through him.

"So now what are you going to do with me?" Her tone had softened measurably even though he could still smell her anger.

"Reckon I could do just about anything I wanted." He drove through Prince George, heading for the highway that would lead out to her place, and to his.

"You could do anything you wanted without tying me up," she pouted.

Images of what he could do to her with her hands tied behind her back, clogged his senses, and he struggled to pay attention to the road. He glanced over at her, her wrists pinned behind her back, and those large breasts stretched against her black sweater. The scent of her cum, rich and intoxicating, filled the cab, and he remembered how wonderful she tasted.

The highway stretched out ahead of them, and he knew he needed to pull over. He would explain to Simone why she had earned her punishment, but he couldn't think with his cock throbbing in his pants. A dirt road that led to some land he leased to local ranchers appeared ahead of them, and he slowed quickly, then turned on to the rough surface.

Simone bounced in the seat, and fell toward him. He grabbed her hair, and held her face pinned to his lap as he slowed the truck to a stop, making sure it was out of sight from any drivers who might pass by.

He put the truck in park, and then ran his hand over the curve of her hip. He would go mad with need for her in this position.

"You are tied up for a reason." He kept his tone quiet, relaxed. "You will learn never to walk away from me during a discussion, and never to run from me."

He doubted she would have learned either if he had forced her to sit in the cab and she remained fuming. He smelled no anger on her now. But the smell of lust racked his senses, making it still hard for him to think.

Maybe some fresh air.

He opened his door, and pulled her outside along with him. Her skirt rode too high on her hips, and the black thong she had on did little to hide her shaven pussy. He half carried her to the back of his truck, and with one hand popped the latches to lower the back door of the truck. He lifted her up and plopped her down so she sat facing him.

"This metal is going to freeze my ass," she told him, her voice no more than a husky whisper.

He liked that she showed no fear. She was as turned on as he was by her punishment. His little bitch was a perfect mix of wild, untamed sensuality, and he didn't want any cruel treatment from pack members to stifle that in her.

"Would you prefer the ground?"

"It depends on what you had in mind."

Her blue eyes glowed at him, a hint of silver streaking through them.

He wanted to talk to her, show her that he approved of how she was, but he couldn't help himself. He shoved her sweater over those distracting mounds of flesh, and squeezed her large breasts. Large brown nipples puckered in the cold, two hardened peaks begging for his attention.

He leaned forward and sucked one of them into his mouth, teasing her nipple with his tongue, tasting her and smelling her lusty scent.

"Hell yes." She tossed her head back, arching into him, and his cock pounded against the material of his jeans, threatening to break through at any moment.

He moved to the other tit, sucking furiously with a need that begged to take over. She moved underneath him, twisting and arching as she fell back and lay on the bed of his truck.

He ran his tongue over her stomach, feeling the burning heat radiate from her sweet-tasting skin. Her breasts filled his hands, and he pinched and twisted her nipples.

"Oh. Shit." Her cries urged him on, as her body writhed under his sweet torment.

Her smooth skin felt hot and he lifted his face to enjoy the view as he stroked her inner thighs, lifting her legs and spreading them. Her black thong was soaked in between her pussy lips, and with a quick motion he yanked the silky material from her body, tossing the tiny piece of lingerie to the ground.

"God. Rock." His actions turned her on. Lust and desire hung in the air, no matter that they were outside and no longer in the confinement of his truck. Her scent would make him wild if he didn't watch himself.

She still showed no signs of fear, but he doubted she was ready for the wild side of him to surface. He needed to maintain control, and keep his Cariboo beast at bay.

Cum soaked her pussy. He spread her legs wide, staring down at the glistening, smooth skin that was the source of the fire that urged him on. His cock ached to be in her. He wanted to hear her scream into the night as he pounded her into sweet submission. But he couldn't. Not yet. He needed to know for sure he had tamed her, made her his, before he could claim and take what he would never give back.

"You have the sweetest pussy." He ran his fingers over it, feeling the humidity soar from inside her. Cum drenched his fingers, fresh and creamy.

"Fuck me, Rock." She didn't ask. She clearly ordered.

He laughed, wanting to do just that.

"Not yet, my little bitch. You aren't ready yet."

"Like hell I'm not." She lifted her ass off the bed of the truck, pressing against his hand. "Fuck me now, damnit."

He speared her pussy with his fingers, diving deep inside her, guided by moist heat. She cried out, spreading her legs and lifting herself up to meet his plunge. She was tight, almost too tight for him, and he wondered when this woman who called herself slut had last been fucked.

He could see her hands, tied together at the wrist, underneath her as she lifted her ass to him. He slipped his fingers from her pussy, and watched fresh cum soak her shaven lips.

Cum dripped to her asshole, and he traced the trail with his finger, and then slid easily inside her. Muscles puckered around his fingers, threatening to suffocate him with burning fire. The heat from her rushed up his arm.

"When were you last fucked?" Both of her holes were so damned tight. He would have to work them a lot before he fucked her. He didn't want to hurt her.

"I...uhh...I'm not sure."

He slid his finger in and out of her ass, her cum making the ride easy. She bucked against his attention, and cried out. He couldn't wait to make her cry out when he drove his cock into her.

"Think, little bitch. I want to know how long it has been. These are not the holes of a slut. You are way too tight."

He stole his attention from her beautiful cum-soaked pussy and ass and met her gaze. She half smiled at him, and he knew she appreciated his comment.

"It's been maybe a month. I don't know." She closed her eyes as he slid deep inside her ass, and then pulled out to circle the cum-soaked, tight little hole with his finger. "But I would like to say that I got fucked tonight. Please. Rock."

He would give in to her pleas if he kept this madness going. He reached for her, longing to enjoy her pussy more, but knowing he only possessed so much strength to control the beast within him, and tonight she wasn't yet ready.

Rock lifted her into his arms, cradling her, absorbing her heat, and her scent. His own desire filled the air with its rich smell too, and he marked her body as best he could with the promise of a commitment.

She lay against him, her bound hands making her helpless in his arms to do more than cuddle against him, and he treasured her compliance, her relaxed body, her willing submissiveness. His little bitch might just train better than he had thought.

Chapter Nine

Simone followed Jere into the country home the following morning. Jere's new preschool was especially for young werewolves. Her daughter would get one on one attention for the first few days, then be allowed to mingle with the other children for short periods after that. This helped keep the young cubs from fighting.

Simone waited until Jere seemed somewhat content playing with the toys before leaving. She had three hours to look for work. And that was her allotted time every morning until she found a job. Jere would be in preschool in the morning, and Simone would spend that time hitting the pavement, looking for a job.

She parked the pale blue Suburban Johann had let her borrow outside the local grocery store, and decided to start by getting a newspaper.

"I didn't know you worked here." Simone smiled at her old friend, Gertrude Rousseau, when she walked up to pay for the newspaper.

"Just one of the jobs I have." Gertrude leaned on a stool behind the checkout counter. "So why did you run out of Howley's the other night?"

Simone dropped the newspaper on the counter and Gertrude rang it up.

"I'm tired of being called a slut, Gerty."

"Well, do you think running with Rock Toubec is going to improve your reputation?"

Simone handed Gerty the change for the paper, and took her time answering.

"I don't know a lot about him...yet." She looked up and met her friend's concerned gaze. "But Gerty, there is something about him. He isn't like any other man I've been with before."

Gerty glanced around the store. It was mid-morning, so Simone guessed that was why the place was free of shoppers.

"He is Cariboo *lunewulf*," she whispered.

"So..." Simone decided she didn't like labels. "And I'm a slut. But I tell you what, I haven't had sex in ages. Guess I'm a pretty lousy slut."

"Simone." Gertrude rolled her eyes. "Rock Toubec is dangerous. The pack is scared of him."

"And you believe pack gossip?"

Gertrude smiled. "Almost never."

Simone picked up her newspaper, and glanced as two old human women entered the grocery store. The automatic doors slid open, and then closed silently behind them. She watched two police cars hurry down the main street, and then turned her attention back to Gertrude.

"I'm not going to base my opinion of him on pack gossip."

Gertrude shrugged. "Well then, don't run every time someone spits old gossip about you in your face."

Her friend was right. If she wanted to overcome the gossip from the pack, she needed to stand up to it.

"I'll keep that in mind." She held up the newspaper. "Wish me luck finding a job."

Simone's heart skipped a beat, and a lump in her throat made it hard to swallow when she approached the Suburban and saw Rock leaning against the front of it. She glanced back toward the large windows of the grocery store, but Gertrude had moved away from her checkout stand. Her friend wouldn't have noticed him standing there.

Rock spoke on his cell phone, and looked her way as she approached. Deep blue eyes speared through her, and her breath caught in her throat. It wasn't a hot day, but a rush of warmth traveled through her. This man displayed more carnal sex appeal than any werewolf she had ever laid eyes on.

He closed his cell phone, and clasped it to his belt, never taking his eyes off of her. His expression remained unreadable, with high cheekbones, and his close shaven beard bordering lips that could damage her piece of mind.

Rock wore a T-shirt, which stretched over bulging chest muscles, and didn't cover thick biceps and when he stuck his thumbs in his jeans' pockets she lowered her gaze to watch the movement. His T-shirt tucked in to snug-fitting jeans, showing off tight abs. Long legs rippled with muscle that the denim couldn't hide. He wore well-worn cowboy boots, and had one boot crossed over the other.

A dangerous werewolf. Raw, untamed masculinity. That was the only way to describe his scent. She stopped in front of him, moist heat saturating her pussy just from being in his presence.

"How did you know it was me driving the Suburban?"

He cocked his head, and took his time letting his gaze travel down, and then back up her body. Her heart began a primitive, slow pounding as she waited out his inspection.

"I didn't. But whoever was driving it would know where you were." He pulled his thumbs from his pockets and crossed his arms over his chest.

Too many muscles bulged in front of her, and her legs grew weak while heat rushed through her, settling in her pussy.

He took in her mini-dress, one of the more modest ones she owned, and her ribbed wool stockings, then her flat-heeled boots.

"What are you doing?" he asked.

It took her a second to hear his question. His presence in front of her invaded her senses. Thinking became a chore she didn't want to endure. More than anything, all she wanted was for him to touch her. She wanted to run her hands over those rippling muscles, feel his strength and unleashed power. Standing in front of Rock could turn her into a blubbering idiot.

"Looking for a job," she managed to say.

Rock didn't comment, but instead reached for her. He was like water to a parched soul. He grabbed her arm and pulled her to him, and his mouth claimed hers before she had a chance to catch her breath.

His tongue attacked her mouth, spearing her with fire that burned with so much intensity she could hardly react. She knew desire, understood lust, but the cravings this man showed her shadowed anything she had experienced before. He dominated, demanded, conquered without resistance. Such raw, aggressive lust was almost too much for her.

His arms snaked around her, slamming her against him and knocking the wind out of her. He held her to him so tightly, breathing almost wasn't an option. Her feet left the ground as he pulled her closer.

She sucked in air when his mouth left hers, but all she did was fill her lungs with the raw, tangy scent that was Rock Toubec. Her skin tingled and her bones popped as lust consumed her and her body craved to change. How wonderful it would be if she could let her beast take over and enjoy such a raw emotion in its purest form.

"I think that ought to do it." Rock straightened, but continued to hold her, looking down at her with turquoise eyes that burned with the same heat she felt in her pussy.

"Ought to do what?" She couldn't focus with fire pulsing in her pussy, her body one solid nerve ending, not to mention his throbbing cock pressing against her belly.

"I need to make sure the other wolves keep their paws off of you." His phone rang, and he looked away from her to answer it.

He needed to make sure of what? She watched the breeze move the curls on his head. Rock focused on his phone call, and not her. His words sounded again in her head.

He had kissed her, turned her insides into molten lava, put her on the verge of exploding right there in the middle of downtown, to make a statement? She glanced around her, noticing the parked cars but not recognizing any of them. A couple of bitches, a bit older than her, probably mated, walked toward them. Each one of them glanced at her, and then at Rock, but continued with their idle chatter and walked by. A car or two passed them. But no one slowed down or made eye contact with her or Rock.

Who was he trying to make a statement to?

And furthermore, did he think her incapable of telling a wolf no?

It dawned on her that Rock must not think any different of her than the rest of the pack. But if he figured she was a slut, why hadn't he fucked her yet?

None of his damned actions made any sense, and she was getting sick of it. She wanted him to spell out what he thought, and why he did what he did, or didn't do. Simone almost laughed out loud. She was expecting this out of a man?

Rock hung up his phone and turned his attention to her. She almost forgot her growing frustration when those turquoise eyes met hers. Unbridled passion gripped her and she couldn't look away. She didn't need to worry about smelling his emotions; she could see them. Anguish spread across his face. His eyes burned with a need that matched the painful craving within her. His mouth pursed into a scowl of control that could only be a result of suppressed desire.

You are making this so much harder than it needs to be.

Maybe he was more affected by the talk of the pack than he admitted. That thought hadn't crossed her mind until now. After all, he was a substantial landowner and successful businessman in the community—a community who viewed Cariboo *lunewulf* as a bit too rough around the collar.

"You can look for a job later." Rock's comment took her by surprise. "Right now you are going home."

"Why am I going home?" She stared at him. The werewolf made no sense. "If you think I can't handle myself out in public without you having to put a mark on me…"

She needed to set this man straight. He thought her incapable of turning a man down. He had asked her not to see any other werewolves, but apparently her word meant little to him.

"This isn't a discussion." Fire burned in those deep blue eyes. "Do as I say, little bitch, or I swear I will hogtie you and throw you in the back of the truck, and take you home myself."

This had gone too far. Cariboo *lunewulf* or not, she wouldn't be verbally abused like this.

She stormed around him, yanking open her truck door. "Let's get one thing straight right now." She stabbed her finger into his iron chest. "I do what I do because it's what I want. I'm not going to take being bossed around like this."

Fury burned inside her, replacing the lust she had felt moments before. And she would be damned if he saw her shaking because she was angry, not because he frightened her.

She plopped onto the driver's seat, but she wasn't ready to leave, not without making damned sure he understood her feelings toward his behavior.

Rock shut her truck door, closing her in, but she rolled the window down as quickly as she could. He had already turned and walked toward his truck, parked several stalls down from her.

"You don't scare me, Rock Toubec," she yelled after him, but he didn't turn around to acknowledge her.

Chapter Ten

Simone pitied all caged animals. She now had first-hand knowledge how they felt. She paced the dark kitchen, stopping to look through the window in the back door, then turned toward the living room.

Samantha and Johann had gone to bed hours ago, and Jere remained cuddled under her blankets. But Simone couldn't sleep.

Two days. She had endured two days cooped up in this house, under orders not to take off anywhere without an escort. And Johann determined he was the only appropriate escort.

Another body had been found on Rock's land. She hadn't heard from him since the day he saw her downtown, and she realized later the phone call he'd received that day was probably informing him of the tragedy.

This body, also female, had been a werewolf. Johann had managed to make connections with a werewolf from the pack south of Prince George, who worked in law enforcement. The bitch had been dead longer than the first human female found, but it appeared her murder had been sexually related as well.

"If he is killing these women, then you are in danger. Don't you see that?" Johann had argued with her earlier.

"The only danger I am in, is in going crazy," she muttered to herself, while remembering their argument earlier. "See? I'm already talking to myself."

She threw her hands up in exasperation, and wished more than anything she could go for a late night run. If she didn't get out of this house soon she would go nuts.

Silence surrounded her, interrupted only by the gentle breathing at the other end of the house from those sleeping. She turned toward the back door.

Several lawn chairs sat in the middle of the backyard, and she relaxed into one while using another for a footrest. Let Johann yell at her for being out here. She wasn't going anywhere, just enjoying the night air.

Stars twinkled against the black sky, but she only focused on them for a second. She stretched out in the two chairs, leaning her head back, and let her thoughts drift toward Rock.

Who are you, Rock Toubec?

A mystery. That's who he was. His sexy good looks, with those dark blue eyes, penetrating and dangerous, watching her, controlling her, manipulating her actions with a simple stare. Her insides warmed thinking of him, and she ran her hands over her body as she arched her back.

Tingles of electricity shot through her where she touched herself, and she arched more, extending her body. She pretended her hands were Rock's hands—large, rough, and skilled.

Her pussy swelled with denied need, and nipples tightened and puckered under her shirt. His kiss downtown the other day had been to ward away other wolves. Did he not think she was interested in him?

That could hardly be the case. She slid her hands inside her jeans and feverish humidity greeted her fingers. Her interest boiled with a raging need.

Did he think he had made her so horny she would turn to the first cock offered her? She ran a finger over the sensitive folds of her smooth pussy, liquid heat clinging to her skin. Her insides clenched, begging for attention, needing the satisfaction her touch could barely offer.

No. Not just any cock would appease the cravings building inside her. One werewolf possessed the skill to soothe her pain. Only one could satisfy the craving that consumed her.

Rock Toubec had sought her out, damnit. He had come on to her. His seductions had started that first night in the meadow when he found her out on a run. Her interest in him may have existed, but he nourished it, encouraged it.

Pressure built to a fiery head when she glided first one finger, and then another, into the silky moistness of her pussy.

"Damn you, Rock." The blackness of the night didn't answer her, but she shook with feverish turmoil, clamping her legs together against her hand. She finger-fucked herself, but there was no relief. No edge taken from the craving her body sought.

The phone inside began ringing and she jumped, yanking her hand out of her jeans, the scent of cum lingering in the air around her. Someone in the house would wake up, and she didn't feel like company at the moment. She darted off the lawn chair, and made it inside the kitchen to grab the phone halfway through its second ring.

"Hello."

"What are you doing?"

His voice surged through her like a tidal wave. She sucked in a long, slow breath and glanced down the hallway of the dark house. Did everyone still sleep? Her heart pounded loudly in her chest and she willed her breathing to relax.

All seemed quiet and she turned to the back door, wondering if she should tell Rock what she had been doing.

"Masturbating." His silence brought a grin to her face.

She slipped out the back door, and returned to her makeshift sanctuary of lawn chairs.

"Why are you masturbating?" His baritone fed the fire burning inside her.

She slid back into her previous position and pressed her hand against her belly, feeling the yearning of her pussy as her fingers traveled slowly toward the moist heat of her cunt.

"Because there is no one here to fuck."

His growl immediately told her she had chosen her words poorly, but she decided he deserved a small amount of agony for the torment her body endured. After all, her physical and mental state was all his fault.

"And you would fuck anyone who came along?"

"Well, right now I'm fucking my fingers." She eased back in the chair, allowing her hand the most room in her jeans, and sucked in her breath when her palm pressed against her swollen clit.

She didn't like his question, and decided she would just let him wonder instead of assure him of her loyalty.

"Little bitch." The frenzied edge to his words forced her heart to beat harder. "Do your fingers satisfy you?"

She cradled the phone against her shoulder, and palmed her breast. Tender and swollen, she craved her nipples to be sucked, wished more than anything her fingers could serve as a hot mouth.

No. Satisfaction wouldn't be obtained tonight. Her frustrations soared with every stroke, every touch, and she couldn't leave herself alone. In spite of the pain, even though fiery need burned inside her, she couldn't stop her fingers.

"My nipples ache, Rock." She pinched one and fire surged through her. "Oh. Damn."

"Shit, baby." The hiss in her ear when he sucked in his breath sent chills through her.

Cum coated the smooth walls of her pussy. She pushed her fingers, forcing them in as deep as they would go. But even wiggling them didn't soothe the molten pressure building deep inside her. The fiery ache only crept through her further, pulsating like a rabid fever.

"I can't reach the spot," she moaned on a ragged whisper, wishing she wouldn't confess her desperation to him, but unable to keep her misery at bay.

"What spot?" His haggard tone egged her on.

"In my pussy, Rock. I'm on fire. I need to be fucked so bad."

"And if Johann came to you right now?" Torment ran through his words. "Would you turn him away?"

She had never turned Johann away. She pulled her fingers from her soaked cunt slowly, feeling the denied lust soar through her. But she hadn't been with Johann for years now, and tonight he hadn't even entered her thoughts.

"Johann?" She couldn't manage a mental image of him, her mind unwilling to let go of her images of Rock. "He wouldn't come to me."

"Damnit to hell, little bitch!" Anger soared through his words, and she jumped at his sudden outcry. "Tell me if you would fuck him or not."

"No, Rock. I don't want Johann." Her admission brought silence. "If he saw me doing what I'm doing right now, I would be embarrassed, but I wouldn't want to fuck him."

Pain and relief appeared tangled when he exhaled, an almost strangled sigh. "Tell me what you are doing."

"I'm pretending my hands are your hands." She pulled her fingers out of her soaked cunt, and spread her thick cream over her smooth pussy lips.

"You're going to come for me."

The confident authority in his tone brought her to the edge. Breathing became a challenge, while her world focused on what her hands were doing, and his voice.

"I could if you were here." Her clit was swollen, a tortured knob that she could hardly touch without electric charges rushing through her.

"I am there. Your hands are my hands." His breathing staggered, and she imagined him stroking that huge cock of his. "Finger-fuck yourself, my bitch. Dive deep into that cunt of yours."

She did as he instructed, her feverish pussy stretching as she pushed deep into the soaked depths of her heat. The air around her hung heavy with her desire, her need to be fulfilled, her longing to be fucked.

"It's not enough." She shoved deep into her pussy, trying to reach the spot that craved attention, the focus of her lust, the point on the verge of exploding.

"Allow a bit of the change, my precious bitch." His words were like her own thoughts, stroking her feverish mind, reassuring and strong, while her body twisted in tortured agony. "I don't want you to hurt yourself, but change just enough to reach that spot."

All she could do was as he instructed. Her mind and body craved his attention, leaned on every word he spoke into her ear.

Her fingers contorted. Small tidal waves rippled through her bones. Lust twisted while carnal and human instinct and thought battled each other. The craving to explode, to reach that orgasm just beyond her human touch consumed her and she stretched her fingers, while moving them in and out of her hot cunt.

"Help me. Rock." Her garbled pants sounded like another person. She barely heard her own words, all of her attention focused on soothing the fire that consumed her senses.

"You're almost there, baby." His pants matched her own, and she saw the huge cock in her mind, his long fingers wrapped around it, stroking up and down.

She matched that stroking beat with her own fingers, longer now and slightly twisted. Extended bones pressed against the fiery walls of her pussy. Humidity soared around her hand while she plunged again and again deep into her cunt, feeling the orgasm near, aching for the explosion he would bring her to.

"I can feel it." With knuckles slightly larger, new sensations rippled through her, egging on her climax, offering hope to the tortured session she endured.

"Tell me how it feels."

She could almost feel his heavy breathing, his voice caressing her enraptured soul, whispering so close, yet so far away. She longed for him to be here, touching her, feeling her climax, watching her explode.

"The pressure. My new shape. Oh." How could she describe the inferno crashing through her? With extended teeth, and a tongue almost too long for speech, she had to work to form the garbled words.

"Fuck your cunt, little bitch. Soak your hand with your sweet juices. Smell your need, and do it for me."

Yes. She could do that. Her fingers dove into her drenched hole, lengthened fingers, with thicker knuckles, pushing against her tender pussy, bringing the flames of desire within her to a peak.

"Shit. Oh. Yes." An explosion of light poured through her. Wave after wave of pent-up lust rushed over the fire in her cunt.

"That's it, baby. You came for me."

"Yes." She breathed the word while her body contorted. Her orgasm soothed the pain, but the longing still remained. "But it's not enough, Rock."

"I will take you soon." His promise tortured her. Adding assurance that he couldn't see her now.

"I'm right here. What are you waiting for?"

"You will wait for me. And when the time is right, I will take you."

She straightened in her seat, pulling her hand from her jeans, her pussy still burning even after her self-induced climax. But instead of satisfaction, she felt an emptiness, desires denied, and only words offered for her to hold on to.

"Until then you will behave, and wait for me," he added.

"Better not make me wait too long, wolf-man." But his end of the phone had gone dead.

Chapter Eleven

Rock wondered if the barbed wire they'd mended would hold through the winter. The men behind him continued their discussion, and he half-paid attention. He didn't deny the seriousness of the issue, but he would handle matters his own way, in spite of what they decided.

"What we want to know, is what investigation you got going on to find out who is dumping these bodies on Toubec's land." Hanson could get riled after a few cups of coffee.

"The coroner's report doesn't indicate they were dumped here." Detective Beuerlein had a soft-spoken manner.

Rock turned away from the window in the large family room that once had been the place all Rousseau pack meetings were held. The large, high-ceilinged room made their voices echo.

"They weren't murdered here." Rock studied the detective's expression, concerned and overworked. The werewolf had a good reputation in law enforcement though, which was why Rock had agreed to this meeting.

"Now how do you know that?" Toby Beuerlein wasn't a big man, most *lunewulf* weren't, but he didn't seem fazed by Rock's size, a trait Rock liked seeing in another wolf—it showed confidence.

"We would have heard the women cry out." Rock glanced out the large bay windows again, the open meadows offering a panoramic view. "More than likely they would never have been murdered."

"So you think someone killed these women, and then brought them here and dumped them off?" Beuerlein rubbed his chin as if considering the possibility.

"We know that is how it was done," Hanson snapped. "Now you got to find out who is doing it."

Beuerlein ignored Hanson's comment. Rock turned again to look at the detective, and saw the man watching him, summing him up, determining the quality of his word, trying to decide if he were a murderer or not.

"You got any enemies, Toubec?"

"I bought the Rousseau ranch for the price of back taxes out from under a family who've had this land in their name for generations."

And not one of them had the intelligence to stop me from doing it. He didn't give a rat's ass about the Rousseau family, nor was he worried about them, but one of them might be stupid enough to pull a stunt like this.

Beuerlein nodded, and continued to watch him. "So you think someone is setting you up."

"I think someone is dropping dead bodies off on my land." No one would frame him for murder. He wouldn't allow it.

Beuerlein stuck his hands in his jacket pocket, and Rock watched him glance from him to Hanson. "I need to talk to Johann. My guess is that this is a pack problem. We've had a good look at those bodies, and although the murders were clean, we're pretty sure one of us killed them. Especially the bitch. Someone knew to break her neck in order to kill her."

"I know this much." Hanson spoke up. "There won't be any other bodies deposited out here. We're watching for them now."

Beuerlein stiffened at the comment. Rock could tell the detective fought to keep emotions at bay by the careful blank expression he kept on his face.

"Do not try to take matters into your own hands, Toubec."

No one told him what to do, but Rock had to admire the wolf for trying. He didn't feel a need to answer, knowing damned good and well he wasn't going to wait for the law to solve this matter. He allowed Hanson to see the detective out, and headed the opposite direction out the back door.

* * * * *

"Never trust a werewolf who is willing to work alongside humans." Hanson joined him several minutes later on the side of one of the larger outbuildings.

Rock focused on the row of pines that sheltered the six small cottages where the first body had been found.

"Nothing wrong with humans." Rock didn't have any working on his ranch. But it wasn't because he didn't trust them. He enjoyed the freedom his land offered, and had been proud to offer work to a handful of Cariboo *lunewulf* who had been struggling back in the mountains.

"You got a plan to find out who dumped those bodies?"

Rock didn't want to think about the murders right now. The whole matter irritated him. A hot little blonde had distracted his thoughts throughout the night, robbing him of sleep. Just thinking about her fucking herself, making herself come while he listened on the phone, masturbating because she wanted to. The little bitch was so fucking hot, and the thought that these murders kept her from him made his blood boil. He needed Simone or he would go nuts.

Ever since he had called her the other night, his cock had been hard. A burning fury raced through him, making it hard to concentrate. The town wasn't safe for bitches right now, especially one as hot as Simone, not until whoever killed those two women was found and killed. He would see to their murder himself. A small price for disturbing his land, and his peace of mind.

"You ain't hearin' a word I'm sayin'," Hanson grumbled.

Rock realized he had started walking across the meadow toward the six cottages he had dreamed about turning into a lodge for werewolves. Hanson struggled to keep the pace, his limp looking more like a staggered trot. Rock stopped and looked down at his ranch manager.

"What did you want?"

"Now don't you take that tone with me." Hanson puffed out his five-gallon barrel chest, and put his hands on his hips. "I don't care if you are eight feet tall, Toubec. You ain't nothing but a pup, and I'll take you down a notch or two if I have to."

If there was one thing Rock had pounded into his head since he was a pup, it was to respect his elders. He turned and continued walking, at a much slower pace so his ranch manager could keep up.

"That little bitch has your cock wrapped around your neck," Hanson muttered.

Rock stopped again, amazed how the old wolf could read his mind.

"I don't know who killed those females. But if they did it out of personal hatred toward me, Simone isn't safe." He wanted her here on the ranch, so he could protect her, and fuck her until she couldn't remember any other werewolf she had ever been with.

His ranch manager stared at him a moment, and this time, he began the walk across the meadow, not commenting.

Rock leaped after him, falling into stride next to the old man. "If there is something you aren't telling me…"

The old wolf's expression turned hard, and he focused ahead looking toward the cottages, and not at Rock.

"You're a good werewolf, Toubec. But I worry they are going to try to take you down."

"Don't worry about the pack, Hanson." Rock couldn't think of a single werewolf in town who wouldn't kiss his ass if he demanded it.

"And now you are sniffing around that little bitch…"

"Yeah. And?"

"And she isn't known for her solid character." Hanson didn't look at him, but entered the grove of pine trees.

"Her past is no longer an issue." Rock cut through the air with his hand, mentally slicing the past away.

"Maybe not for you. But what if she can't change the way you want her to?"

Rock didn't like where this conversation was headed. He wouldn't think about Simone lusting after some other wolf. The thought made his blood boil. She was on the wild side, but he could tame her. No other werewolf would touch her and live through it.

"She doesn't like the way people talk about her." And he knew she wasn't encouraging the talk. Ever since he'd met her, he knew she wasn't dating around, or sleeping around. She was always at home. "If she ran in the meadow with a few wolves when she was younger, that's fine. She isn't doing it now."

"Now you know I've been in this area for a long time. This is my pack, and I know these werewolves."

They entered the clearing and Rock stared at the row of cottages, desperately in need of repair. He thought about bringing Simone out here, showing her around the place. He could see her sexy walk in front of him, her adorable ass swaying from side to side while she checked out each cabin. She would love it out here. The privacy. The quiet.

"Make your point, Hanson." He was about ready to tell his ranch manager to get back to work and leave him be.

"I remember her running with the other wolves and bitches her age. I used to get out more than I do now, you know. And I tell you this, Toubec. Your biggest worry is right under that roof where she is staying."

Rock focused on his mental image of Simone, those wonderful large breasts. God, he wanted to tease and torture those nipples until she screamed in ecstasy. He wanted her naked, and on her knees before him, sucking on his cock, while she watched him with her sultry baby blue eyes.

But his image slowly faded as Hanson's words hit him. He turned and stared at his ranch manager, meeting the man's hard gaze.

"Are you suggesting she isn't safe where she is staying?"

"Depends on what you call safe." Hanson slapped his pockets, as if searching for something.

Rock realized the man was hesitating, searching for how to say something, or not wanting to say it at all.

"You're damned determined to tell me something." Grouchiness suddenly surged through him. There was work to be done, damnit. "You didn't follow me out here because you have nothing to do."

Hanson looked offended, and turned to leave, but then turned right back around again, and pointed a finger at him.

"Simone De Beaux got her reputation as a slut because she was always fucking that new pack leader. And she wasn't his bitch. He wanted that little Rousseau bitch. And that little bitch of yours had her own three mates assigned to her. But they wouldn't touch her because she was Johann's slut. Mighty convenient for him to be housed up with his mate, and still have Simone under his roof as well."

Fire burned through Rock faster than he could control it. Blind rage consumed him, and he barely noticed the old wolf stumble backwards. He heard his shirt rip, while bones popped and contorted. His spine lengthened, pulling muscles inside him, stretching and altering their shape.

Ripples of fury over the blasphemous statement of his own hired help burned through his soul. Simone was not

Johann's slut. How dare the old wolf imply such a thing! He would kill Johann, kill the old wolf, kill anyone who dared to hazard slander against his bitch.

Rock stumbled backward, his legs no longer shaped to hold him upright. He wanted to swipe the air with his long claws, shred anything he could make contact with. Tear and destroy until his temper bayed.

His mouth lengthened, and teeth grew, pressing against his gums, forcing their way out until they resembled lethal weapons. Raw power of the beast who was part of him, pumped through his blood, speeding up his heartbeat, primal instinct consuming all rational thought.

He leaned his head back and howled, screamed in outrage, letting his anger consume him, take over as the beast within him had. Simone wanted him. He knew that she did. Hadn't she masturbated for him over the phone just the other night? Her cry was for him. She came and fucked herself for him.

He wouldn't accept the fact that she would howl for another wolf. He had seen her need in her eyes. She wanted him, damnit, not the fucking pack leader.

Rational thought seeped through him like molasses. Torturously slow, and fighting an uphill battle as carnal rage ripped through him.

The urge to fall to all fours and tear across his land, not stopping until he had that little bitch in tow, and then bringing her home with him, about killed his ability to think straight. But what would that accomplish? Taking her by force appealed to him rather nicely, but behavior like that would only bring him trouble.

Rock forced his breathing to slow, fought to ease the pace of the blood that surged through him, and straightened while bones popped back into their human form.

"This is how the pack thinks." He heard Hanson's words, and turned to see the old wolf holding his hand over his heart.

Rock reached up and ripped a small branch from one of the trees, and hurled it across the open area in front of them. There was no satisfaction in the act. He watched the branch fly through the air, and then slide along the ground toward the end of the row of cottages.

"Pack leader or not, if Johann Rousseau lays one paw on her, I will kill him." Rock turned and headed back toward the house, not bothering to slow his pace so the ranch manager could keep up, and no longer in the mood to dream about his werewolf retreat.

Chapter Twelve

Simone hurried into her bedroom and searched through the boxes on the floor, looking for Jere's jacket.

"Hurry up. This outing is going to turn into a day's event." Johann's grouchiness over taking them shopping didn't sway her mood in the least.

"No one is forcing you to go with us." She entered the living room with her daughter's jacket in hand, and reached for Jere.

Johann held their daughter in his arms and took the jacket, instead of handing the cub to her.

"Let's go."

Simone smiled at her daughter, who looked as excited as she was to get out of the house, even if they had to endure the sour attitude of Johann for the day. She hadn't left the house all week, other than to drive with Johann and Samantha every morning to take Jere to preschool and then to pick her up. The thought of actually getting out and doing something thrilled her enough to overcome Johann's grouchiness.

Although she doubted Rock would go to a clothing store, she couldn't give up hope that she might possibly see him while out today. He hadn't called since the other night, and she hadn't found a moment to herself in order to call him.

"I want to get a new doll, Mommy." Jere sat in the back seat next to Simone, with the seat belt strapped around her. "Will you make Daddy buy a doll for me?"

Samantha turned around, grinning at Jere. "If you're very good while we're out, maybe we will let you pick out a doll."

"What you really need are school clothes." Simone tapped her daughter's nose.

"I want both, Mommy."

Johann drove them into town, all of them chatting easily, keeping the topic light. Simone couldn't keep her thoughts off Rock though. It would be so wonderful to see him, even if she could just get an eyeful of that sexy body she'd been dreaming about the past few nights.

By the time they reached the shopping area, her nerves were in a frenzy. Her heart pounded when she got out of the car, unable to stop herself from glancing around for Rock's truck.

Jere undid her own seatbelt, and crawled across the seat to get out next to Simone. She held her daughter's hand, following Samantha and Johann into the store, but continued to search the area for any sign of that overgrown werewolf who continued to haunt her dreams.

"You look tired." Simone noticed Samantha had lost her enthusiasm a couple hours later. "Johann, we need to find a place to sit and rest a while."

Johann turned and eyed his mate. "How about we go have some lunch?"

"Are you in the mood for a cheeseburger?" Simone had her answer when Samantha's expression lit up.

"Yes. With all the fixings." She rubbed her hands together.

"Let's take her to Howley's." Simone wondered if by chance Rock knew of the excellent food served there. "She hasn't had a chance to try their food yet."

Thirty minutes later, Simone carried Jere to a booth inside her old hangout. The lunch crowd had assembled, and she wasn't surprised to see a fair amount of the pack still frequented the place over the noon hour.

"So, you have finally come back to your pack." A man's voice startled her, and Simone looked up from helping Jere take her new doll out of the packaging.

"Well hello, Armand." She smiled up at the stocky werewolf, and then returned her attention to undoing the wires that fastened the doll to her plastic encasing.

Armand Gaston slipped into the booth opposite her, and she chanced a glance toward the bar, where Johann and Samantha were surrounded by several werewolves and engrossed in conversation.

"Still under Rousseau's protection?" Armand followed her gaze toward Johann.

"He is pack leader, Armand. That is the only protection he is offering."

"Well, that is good news. I take it that means you are no longer sniffing after the wolf? He seems to have a nice bitch for a mate."

"Samantha is wonderful." She had no desire to discuss her sexual life with this wolf, and wished like hell that Johann and Samantha would join them over here. "The two of them make a wonderful couple."

"Good. Very good." Armand leaned back and tapped his stubby fingers on the table. "I thought it best to let you know beforehand. But I will make a formal appointment with Johann in order to secure you as a mate."

"What?" Simone gasped, almost dropping Jere's doll.

Her daughter struggled to help her mother get the final wires off the doll's wrist, and Simone let her take over the project.

"I have no intention of being your mate," she added, recovering somewhat from the audacity of his statement.

"My dear bitch. You already are my mate." Armand Gaston crossed his arms over his chest, looking very pleased with himself. "But I am looking forward to making it official."

She almost cringed when his gaze dropped to her breasts, and she swore he appeared to be drooling.

"What are you talking about?" But then it hit her.

Several stapled pieces of paper. And so many years ago she had almost forgotten the list. Grandmother Rousseau's treacherous list. She remembered the foggy morning when she had sat, recovering from a hangover, and read over the list stating the werewolves who would be mated with the bitches. Armand Gaston was one of her three mates.

Her tongue suddenly felt like sandpaper. Armand reached across the table and put his sweaty, thick hand over her clasped hands. The urge to bolt raced through her like a volt of electricity. It took more power than she thought she had to sit there and appear unnerved by his words.

"You're being ridiculous." She fought the pounding of her heart, and hoped she sounded in control. If this man's brassy claim upset Jere, she would bitch-slap him right here in the bar. "Grandmother is dead, and that law was preposterous anyway."

"But, my dear, it's still a law, and on the books. I have a right to you."

Simone jumped up from the booth, fury and panic swarming through her. The air around her seemed too thin suddenly, and she worked several slow, calming breaths doing her best to maintain control in front of her daughter. This werewolf had more nerve than should be allowed for such a stocky runt. She wanted to pound some sense into his dense head.

Jere grabbed her doll and slid across the booth toward her. "Where are we going, Mommy?"

She noticed her daughter's worried expression, and realized Jere detected her outrage in the air. "It's okay, sweetheart." She lifted her into her arms, nuzzling her hair.

"Let me hold her." Armand stood as well, a stupid smile plastered on his face that she would have loved to slap right off of him. "She needs to get used to me."

Simone turned, putting distance between the werewolf and her daughter.

"No. She does not," she hissed. "There is not going to be any mating."

The best thing to do would be to join Samantha and Johann before she lost her cool right here in the middle of Howley's with her daughter in her arms. What a way to make sure everyone knew she was back in town! She glared at the pompous werewolf and headed across the bar.

"We are already mated, bitch. All that is left is the good part." He slapped her ass before she could get away.

Simone screeched. Jere yelped, wrapping her small arms tightly around Simone's neck. Several people in the bar turned. Pack members smiled, not thinking twice of someone harassing her. Simone wanted to scream at the whole lot of them that she deserved some respect.

And what for? Haven't you earned the reputation that you have? Respect is earned too.

Well she would earn this fucking pack's respect if it killed them, she decided. She held her head high, refusing to look at anyone in the bar, and carried her daughter with what she hoped was a small amount of dignity, across the large poolroom to where Johann and Samantha stood.

"Someone giving you trouble?" Johann glanced over her shoulder, but only seemed mildly concerned.

It was best to make light of it, she decided. The only way she could make these people see that she had no intention of fucking every werewolf in the pack, was to not remind them of her past any more than necessary.

"Nothing I couldn't handle." She smiled, handing Jere over to Johann. Her daughter held her new doll in front of her face, half hiding, half showing off her new possession to the few werewolves surrounding them.

Samantha seemed the only one not impressed with her forced cheeriness. "Is everything okay?" she whispered.

Simone nodded, this not being the place to confide her predicament. Although it wasn't a problem. She would see to it that it wasn't a problem. If only Rock were here. But if he were, he would make his presence known. The wolf dominated wherever he went.

And since when did you want a werewolf dominating your life?

The night he tied her wrists in the back of his truck, making her his captive while he enjoyed her body, was proof of how aggressive and dominating Rock could be. His punishment for her walking away from him still preoccupied her thoughts. He wouldn't take bullshit from anyone.

She followed everyone to a large table, where several other pack members joined them for lunch. There were two other werewolves out there who, by pack law, were her mates. The thought of any of the three of them causing her further trouble made it hard to eat. What would Rock do when he learned she was supposed to be mated to three other werewolves? The possibilities made her sick to her stomach.

The worst part about it, she would realize later that night, while she lay in bed staring at the ceiling, was that she couldn't remember the names of the other two mates assigned to her. She needed to know who they were, and then find out if they were in town too. Hopefully they had left the pack, so they could take mates elsewhere.

* * * * *

Jere grew restless an hour later, discussion around the table continuing about pack issues.

"I need to get her out of here." Simone leaned into Samantha to whisper, her friend nodding agreement, while Jere tried to crawl under the table.

Samantha whispered to Johann, while Simone scooped her daughter off the floor. The two of them excused themselves, then followed the excited cub outside.

"Why did you look so upset earlier?" The two of them strolled downtown, glancing in shop windows, while Jere skipped happily in front of them.

"Johann needs to get rid of that law that bound females to three mates." She needed to talk to him about that soon, too.

"One of your three mates confronted you?"

Simone nodded. "He claims I'm his mate, and he plans to try to get it enforced."

"Oh shit." Samantha rested her hand on her growing belly.

"What really worries me is how Rock will react if he finds out by pack law I am mated." She shivered from the thought. "And not just mated to one werewolf, but to three."

"Speak of the devil." Samantha nodded her head, and Simone spun around, her heart flying to her throat.

"I've got to go talk to him." Heated desire clenched her insides when she noticed Rock Toubec get out of his truck at the end of the block. "Will you keep an eye on Jere?"

Samantha grabbed her arm. "You can't just go prancing over there to him."

"Why not?" She watched him close his truck door, the same truck he had bound her in, and walk to the sidewalk, his back to them. Panic crept through her. She hadn't seen him in days, and didn't want to let him get away.

"You've got to make him come to you," Samantha hissed, pulling harder on her arm.

Frustration clamped down on her heart, forming a pain in her chest that made it hard to breathe. He was going to get away. "He doesn't see me. What do you want me to do? Whistle for him?"

Samantha laughed. "You'd get every stray wolf on the block that way. Why don't we just start walking in that direction?"

Simone would have preferred to jog. Rock had disappeared into a hardware store on the corner of the block, but he was in there. And she had to see him. Even if all she could do was say hi, make sure he hadn't forgotten about her. She had prayed all day for the chance to run into him, and she couldn't let this opportunity slip through her fingers.

"Hi ladies." Gertrude crossed the street, smiling. "Any luck finding work, Simone?"

Her friend wore a sweatshirt with the logo of the grocery store where she worked, but carried a bucket of cleaning supplies that bounced against her leg as she walked.

"Have you met Samantha?" Simone quickly made introductions, allowing Gertrude to fuss over Jere for a moment. "And, no. I haven't been allowed out of the house since that second female was found murdered."

She didn't want to be having this conversation. Her attention was focused on that hardware store. Thoughts of that massive werewolf, his brooding gaze determining her feelings, had her insides clamoring to a boiling point.

"I guess that is the only plus side to being mated. I have more freedom." Gertrude lifted her bucket, gesturing with it. "Or at least I am free to work until I drop."

The door to Howley's opened, Johann and a group of other wolves emerging on to the street. He spotted them, and turned in their direction.

Simone noticed Gertrude sag and groan at the same time. "Well hell," she muttered. She turned to Simone, reaching with her free hand, and squeezing Simone's arm. "Let's get together and chat sometime. Right now, I've got to get out of here. The last thing I want is to be cornered by my mate right now."

Her old high school friend hurried off, offering no further explanation.

"Sounds like you aren't the only one who doesn't like that law," Samantha muttered before Johann reached them.

There was no way Simone could tell Johann she wanted to hang around so she could see Rock. But she couldn't let him herd them away without having an opportunity to talk to him. Longing rattled through her, making it hard to think.

"I'll be right back." She hurried after Gertrude, before Johann or Samantha could utter a protest.

Chapter Thirteen

Gertrude was her only hope. She could remain prisoner under Johann's roof for God only knew how long if she didn't act quickly.

"Gerty, wait up." Her friend was already halfway down the block.

"Don't tell me you want to help me clean offices." Gertrude turned toward a door leading to an accounting firm.

"Well, I might." Simone glanced past her, willing the door to the hardware store to open, and Rock to appear.

"Trust me. There is no glamour to it. And after this I get to clean Matthew's office. Since he's my mate, I don't get paid for that one." She rolled her eyes, fishing through her pocket at the same time. She pulled out a keychain weighed down with keys.

Simone had to keep the conversation going, anything to keep Gertrude on the street just a minute or two longer. "You don't sound like you are too happy with your mates. Are you still with all three?"

How long could a visit to a hardware store possibly take?

"Don't get me started." Gertrude struggled with her keys, and Simone reached for the bucket. Her friend smiled her thanks. "I'll tell you this much." She hushed her tone. "You would think with three mates I would have something to go home to."

Samantha hurried up to the two of them, and grabbed Simone's arm. "I told Johann I was coming to get you." Her worried expression tied Simone's stomach in a knot. "But Simone, some wolf is talking to him about you. Isn't he the one who bugged you before we ate?"

This couldn't be happening. Armand Gaston stood down the street talking to Johann, who appeared to be listening with interest.

"There is no way I am going down there right now." She wanted to grab her daughter and run, but Johann held Jere, while he nodded, and listened to Armand.

"What's going on?" Gertrude pushed open the office door with her foot, but looked down the street. "Is that Armand that Johann is talking to?"

"He is trying to get Johann to uphold pack law that says he is my mate." Simone watched in horror when Johann started nodding, and then the two of them looked her way. "If Johann sticks to that nasty law Grandmother Rousseau made, I swear I will run again."

Her insides churned frantically when Armand looked like he would walk in her direction. She looked the other way, desperate for Rock to appear, but his truck remained parked where it was, no sign of the wolf anywhere.

"Do you think he will dissolve it?" The ring of hope in Gertrude's tone couldn't be missed.

Simone urged Gertrude inside the office building. "Let me clean with you. I can't let these werewolves corner me." She needed a moment to think, knowing she would have to deal with an argument later from Johann, but not caring. "Samantha. Please. Tell Johann I'm working with Gertrude. He can't argue that I need a job."

"We can lock ourselves in here." Fortunately, Gertrude seemed willing to help.

But Samantha looked worried. Simone grabbed her hand and squeezed it, needing her friend to understand her predicament.

"Tell Jere I will be home soon." She smiled into her friend's troubled eyes. "I can't allow myself to get tied into a mating that will make my daughter and me miserable. Please understand."

Samantha nodded, squeezing her hand. "Okay. But please be careful."

An hour later, Simone didn't know what else to offer to do, other than stand and watch Gertrude clean.

"Are you sure I can't do more than empty trash cans?" She glanced around the dimly lit lobby of the accounting firm, with several adjoining offices.

"Seriously. I dust everything and then vacuum. I won't be much longer."

"Well, maybe I'll wonder around outside a bit." She noticed Gertrude's quick questioning glance, but ignored it. "I'll be fine. I only needed to get away earlier so there wouldn't be a scene in front of Jere."

"It's not like the old days, is it?" Gertrude moved items off a desk, and sprayed it with a lemon-scented spray. "We took care of our own then. No one had to run from a wolf."

"The law is on his side. That's the problem." Simone started toward the door.

"Well, it's a fucked up law."

Simone couldn't have agreed more. It wasn't right that a good bitch like Gertrude was miserable with three werewolves. But it was more incentive not to let herself fall into the same predicament. Johann would change the law, more than likely at the next pack meeting. But until then, she needed to steer clear of the three werewolves who had been assigned as her mates. Armand wasn't a worry on his own, but if he sought out help...well the last thing she wanted was to be gang-raped.

On her own, without Johann or Jere to worry about, keeping out of the paws of unwanted attention would be a cinch. She could use the phone in Howley's, and she would call Rock. He had said she would be his. And now she would hold him true to his word.

"What do you mean you don't know where he is?" She glared at the row of clean glasses opposite her, while sitting on a barstool inside Howley's a few minutes later. "You're the ranch manager, or that is what you said when you answered the phone. Why don't you know where Rock is?"

"Don't you get sassy with me, bitch. I remember when you were in pigtails and climbing trees with your tail hanging out."

Simone couldn't place who the ranch manager might be from his voice on the phone, nor did she remember ever climbing trees.

"Ok. Listen." The thumping music in the bar began to grate on her nerves. "Contact your boss. Tell him Simone needs his help. I'm at Howley's."

He grunted and then hung up on her.

Great. Just great.

She couldn't hang out at Howley's indefinitely. Maybe Rock was still downtown somewhere. Sunlight warmed her when she pushed open the large wooden door to the bar, and stepped outside.

If only she had stalled Gertrude a bit longer before they entered to clean that office. Or maybe if she had come outside a bit sooner. She stared at the stall where Rock's truck had been parked, empty stalls surrounding it for a good half a block.

Walls of glass windows filled with tempting displays distracted her. A few shops down she stopped to investigate headless mannequins dressed in schoolgirl outfits. Jere would look so adorable wearing new dresses to school every day.

"I see you've freed yourself of your keeper and your daughter." Armand Gaston strolled toward her, hands stuffed in his pockets.

"Go away, Armand." She hoped her expression appeared bored, because inside her heart began pounding, feeling anything but bored.

"You better be nice to me, bitch. In fact, I have hopes of you being real nice." Armand stopped inches away from her, reeking of onions.

"Fuck off." She wanted to run, wanted to change enough to slap the cocky grin off his face with a few extended claws.

"Fucking is exactly what I had in mind." The leer in his tone couldn't be missed.

"Dream on, wolf-man." She turned to face him, anger building inside her. "Your suggestion is preposterous. Now go away!"

He pulled his hands out of his pocket, putting her senses on full alert. Blood rushed through her, the change building inside her if she needed some muscle.

"A bit jumpy?" Armand laughed. He leaned into her, meeting her eye to eye.

She hated short men.

"You don't impress me enough to get any reaction out of me." She would go back to the bar. She couldn't go back to Gertrude with Armand on her tail.

"Fucking you by force has its appeal too." He grabbed her arm when she tried to walk around him.

His hands were sweaty, the moistness of his grip making her skin crawl. Her heart pounded now, blood surging through her veins, outrage consuming her.

"I doubt you have a cock big enough to even interest me." She spat her words at him, enjoying the cruelty of them.

How dare this werewolf confront her like this!

His fingers slid around her arm, his sweat saturating her skin, curdling her blood, making her want to puke. His grip tightened, and he tried to pull her to him.

"You better watch your mouth, bitch." His eyes narrowed, crow's feet tracing lines to the edge of his face. "I could make you my mate within the next thirty minutes."

"Is that all the time you can last?" She fought to pull her arm free.

A couple of shoppers passed them, giving curious looks but not saying anything.

"You would bore me to death," she added, when the humans were out of earshot.

She yanked her arm free. At least inside Howley's there would be fewer humans. The bartender would be werewolf, and she could make him call Rock.

But if there is a pack problem, he will call Johann.

She stormed toward the bar and grill. All her life she had managed her problems on her own. No one had ever been there to help her. If Rock wouldn't come, this time would be no different than any other. She could take care of herself. She always had, and today would be no different.

It would be so nice to have someone in my corner though.

The darker atmosphere inside Howley's made her hesitate for a second. Several men at the bar turned and gave her the once over. She snarled at them, piquing their interest.

Damn. She needed to get a grip on her actions. This wasn't a new situation for her. So many months spent with Elsa and Rick under their protection, and now with thoughts of Rock, she had grown lazy. Her instincts weren't fine-tuned.

How many times had she warded off an unwanted fuck? Armand Gaston was a wimp, a spineless, overfed werewolf. She had lived through aggressors twice his size. No one would fuck her unless she wished it.

Calm, slow breaths soothed her blood flow. Her heart relaxed in her chest. Muscles throughout her body softened, and she strolled to the bar, making eye contact with each werewolf who sat there.

But Armand was right on her heel. There was no time for idle chatter. She turned on him before he could speak.

"I thought I told you to leave me alone." She put her hands on her hips, doing her best to look like a scolding mother.

His beady blue eyes glanced down the row of local riffraff, enjoying a brew before going home to their mates, or not having anyone to go home to. She didn't have to follow his gaze to know none of them would interfere. The interaction between mated werewolves was personal.

But we aren't mated.

"I have no intention of leaving you alone. You are my mate by law, and we are going to make that official, by force or willingness, your call." He pressed into her, trapping her against the bar.

"I choose neither. Get that through your pea-sized brain." She shoved against his chest with all her might, deciding a show of anger in the establishment would likely make him hesitate. "Or are you thinking with your other head? If that's the case, then we are in trouble since I'm sure your dick is smaller than your brain."

He tried to stop her, but she put muscle into it and pushed him away from her. Outrage turned his cheeks red, the color streaking down his neck. Or was it embarrassment? She didn't care. He brought his own humiliation on himself.

"You need to learn a little respect." He tried to grab her, but enough was enough.

The door opened, and Gertrude entered at the same time she slapped Armand across the face, her nails extended slightly out of anger. Bright puffy lines of red appeared on his cheek, giving her a warm feeling of satisfaction.

"I don't need to learn shit from you." The look of shock that she had just slapped him fed her confidence. "Now, are you going to show a bit of respect, and drop this foolish notion of yours?"

Gertrude edged nearer, looking concerned but possibly amused. "You need a ride home?"

"Sure. There isn't anything here to entertain me." The adrenaline pumped through her though, making her legs a bit shaky when she turned from Armand.

"I'm not through with you." This time when Armand grabbed her arm it hurt. He pulled her side up against his chest, onion breath clogging her lungs. "You are leaving with me. I've talked to our pack leader already, verified the law is intact. You are mine, bitch, whether you like it or not."

Panic about made her choke. Johann wouldn't consent to this dim-witted werewolf mating her, would he?

Gertrude moved closer, touching her, her cool fingers burning Simone's arm. She would not be trapped. No one would tell her what she could or could not do.

"Let's go." Gertrude's voice sounded far away.

Fire seared through her blood, outrage mixing with panic. Every time she inhaled, all she smelled was Armand, onions, determination, and lust. She wanted to puke, spit in his face, rip her arm from his grasp. But he held her tight, pulling, his sweaty grip making her skin itch.

"I don't give a rat's ass about a pack law that will no longer exist by the next pack meeting." She hated him for making her so mad. "Now get your fucking paws off of me."

She pulled with all her strength, muscles growing in her, survival instincts beckoning the change. Her footing wasn't steady. Armand was dragging her toward the door, forcing her to go with him.

She pulled her arm from Gertrude's cool grasp, and formed a fist, ready to punch that determined look off of

Armand's face. The man was insane. There was no reasoning with him.

Sunlight flooded the room. The front door to Howley's opened with a bang. A figure, larger than life, entered the bar. She couldn't focus quickly enough. But all the nauseating smells of Armand suddenly disappeared.

Fury filled her nostrils, carnal rage, dangerous, terrifying. But she didn't feel fear in response. Her insides danced with a new power. Triumphant. Adrenaline poured through her. Every bit of strength she possessed aided her, seemed to come to life. She fought to get free of Armand's hold on her, dragging him toward her.

"Get your fucking hands off of her." Rock Toubec bellowed loud enough for everyone in the bar to hear.

Armand let go. It took a moment to regain her balance. She stumbled a minute but then turned quickly, not wanting to miss Rock knock the tar out of Armand Gaston.

"I've got the law on my side." Armand scurried around a few tables, running like a puny coward.

She about yelled at Armand, telling him just what she thought of him, making sure Rock knew what a weasel he was. But her words choked her, when large hands, hands twice the size of Armand's, lifted her from the ground, and threw her toward the door.

"Get your fucking ass out to the truck. Now!"

She didn't question the order. Pure rage surrounded her. She hurried out of the bar, not bothering to look back to see what would happen next.

Chapter Fourteen

Rock didn't speak while he drove. His anger filled the cab of the car, and Simone decided it would be in her best interest to not ask why he was still so mad. She also didn't question why he was taking her to his place.

The tires of the truck skidded on the gravel when he stopped behind the ranch house. She managed to get her door open, but Rock's long strides around the front of the cab blocked her exit.

His grip on her wrist almost cut off her circulation.

"I'm coming." She tried to steady herself, but he pulled her from the truck, slamming the door behind her.

She couldn't keep up with his long strides, but he didn't seem to notice her half-stumble, half-run next to him as he dragged her into his house.

"Daddy's home." An excited voice shrilled out, and she noticed two cubs sitting at a kitchen table, eating.

"Is that our new mommy?" The other cub, all freckles and a mess of reddish blond hair, looked at her with large blue eyes.

"He has to mate her first, stupid."

Rock ignored his children, not saying a word even to the surprised older woman who stood at the counter, cooking something. Simone didn't have time to look. She stumbled past the family setting, Rock's grip on her wrist unrelenting.

Climbing the stairs proved almost impossible with his hold on her. The carpet burned through her jeans more than once when she stumbled, and then was dragged up the remaining stairs.

"I'll follow you. Don't worry. You don't have to drag me." She barely got her footing at the top of the stairs and almost went to her knees again.

She used her one free hand to keep herself from falling, then tripped over her own feet at his side. He pushed open a door halfway down the hallway, pulling her into a large, airy bedroom.

He released her, but then pushed her forward.

"Get out of your clothes." His baritone ran over her like hot wax.

After being dragged through his house and thrown into his bedroom, it took a minute to get her bearings. She had never experienced such aggression, such domination, such raw, carnal power.

She could still feel his grip on her wrist. Her insides burned from the intensity of his actions, her breath came in staggered gasps, while warmth crept through her, making her pussy throb with anticipation.

Her legs wobbled underneath her when she turned to face him, and she braced them against a bed large enough for an orgy. But when she met his gaze, she forgot to breathe. Cobalt blue eyes burned through her, leaving her breathless, weak with need. He stared at her, his energy filling the space between them. Anger, passion, hunger.

"I told you to take your clothes off." He didn't give her a chance to move, but grabbed the center of her sweater, her breasts rubbing against the material.

"Sounds good to me." She wanted to sound enticing, but her heart pounded a mile a minute, making her feel jittery.

Rock had never seemed so...so aggressive, so possessed. Excitement at being alone with him in his bedroom mixed with nervous energy over the intensity of the emotions that billowed off of him.

He yanked at her sweater, pulling it over her head, before she could take it off of herself. He tossed it behind him, abandoning it while his gaze intensified on her, feeding the fire that burned deep inside her cunt.

Dark blue eyes focused on her breasts, but only for a moment. He scanned her half-naked body, but then met her gaze, his expression masked, waiting, watching.

His mood confused her. And the best thing to do would be to get out of her clothes as quickly as possible. He didn't seem enthused about being seduced. She couldn't stand and take off her boots, at least not without risking falling on her ass. She rested against the edge of his bed, pulled her boots off, then unzipped her jeans and slid them down her legs.

His expression hadn't changed when she stood, naked before him, wondering if she should approach him, or just stand there.

He didn't give her time to ponder the matter.

Rock grabbed her by the shoulder, allowing her to walk this time, as he escorted her to an adjoining bathroom. His shove wasn't gentle though, when he pushed her inside.

"Shower."

She stumbled into bathroom, grabbing the counter to keep from falling. Why was he still so angry?

"You want me to shower?" Her insides knotted with confusion.

"I don't think I can stand another minute of smelling that werewolf on you."

He slammed the door, leaving her alone in the bathroom, and she heard the outer door to his bedroom close as well.

When Simone stepped out of the bathroom, her hair damp from the shower, the bedroom was empty, and her clothes were gone.

Did he expect her to remain naked in his home?

That was hardly acceptable with children around. Rock Toubec needed some taming, and some training. The werewolf was wild, completely out of control. And her pussy swelled with need for him.

She wouldn't be able to find the wolf if she was bare-ass naked. Her feet sank into a thick area carpet as she walked to the other side of his room, then pulled open double doors.

"What kind of wolf are you, Rock Toubec?" She stared at the large closet, clothes hanging on either side. Everything in perfect order.

She pictured the small bedroom she shared with her daughter, their clothes still in boxes. If this closet were indication of Rock's personal hygiene, he would have a fit at the sight of her bedroom.

Like he will ever see the bedroom you have in Johann's house.

T-shirts were folded neatly on a shelf underneath the clothes on hangers. She took the top one, and closed the closet door behind her. Now to find this perfect werewolf.

The T-shirt hung past her knees, serving nicely to cover herself. Her nipples hardened against the material, the thought of wearing his clothes building a pressure deep inside her womb. His bitch. She liked the sound of that.

His bedroom door opened silently, but she froze in the doorway. Rock had reached the top of the stairs, but stopped moving when he noticed her.

Gone was the anger, the outrage, the fury. Beautiful dark blue eyes stared at her, pinning her where she stood, capturing her like a fawn trapped in headlights.

"Why are you dressed?" He approached her slowly, his expression calm, a similar T-shirt stretching over broad shoulders, outlining a perfectly sculptured chest.

"Well, I couldn't come find you naked." She backed up into his room, unable to take her gaze from his. "And my clothes seemed to have disappeared."

"Quinnie is washing them. They stunk." He backed her to the edge of his bed. "But you smell much better."

"Who is Quinnie?" She touched his steel chest, feeling his muscles quiver underneath her hands.

"She is my cousin. She lives here with me, takes care of the boys and the house."

His hands cupped her cheeks, the warmth from them over-stimulating her brain. Long, thick fingers, hard and calloused, slid through her damp hair, pulling her head back, arching her neck as she looked up at him.

She couldn't see around him, but knew the door remained open. His family was downstairs. If only she could touch him, feel that cock she knew must be hard, experience such incredible power with her own hand. Cobalt blue eyes swarmed with lust, his gaze dark and penetrating, making her weak with a craving only he could satisfy.

"She has taken them for a run." He must have read her thoughts.

"Then we are alone." Her heart skipped a beat with pleasure, excitement sending chills over her warm body.

She ran her fingers down his shirt, tracing a pattern with her fingernails, feeling his muscles jerk under her touch, watching his jawline harden, knowing her touch affected him, and enjoying the torment she saw in his gaze.

She didn't stop at his belt buckle, but spread her hand over his jeans, stretching her fingers over his cock, feeling heat from his erection through the thick material. Her mouth went dry, her breathing quickened. The shaft under her hand moved, and she gripped it, curling her fingers into his jeans, testing his size, feeling his strength, daring to stare into the raw power standing over her.

Her fingers stretched over his length, so huge, so thick, just like the werewolf. Everything about him was overgrown. She smiled up at him, doing her best to squeeze his cock through his jeans.

"I think we should both get undressed." Confidence rang through her, and she brushed her nipples against his T-shirt, the roughness tickling her breasts, and saturating her pussy with cum.

"This will not be your day to play." His words were a growl, a hard whisper, chilling her blood.

She didn't understand what he meant, but had no time to question him. He gripped her hair, his hands forming fists on either side of her head, the pinch of pain as he pulled her hair back sending streamlines of excitement straight to her throbbing cunt.

He bent over her, lowering his head, his eyelids dropping over eyes that now glowed with a silver streak. His presence consumed her, filling her space, his body everywhere, muscles harder than steel pressing into her. Everything that was Rock overloaded her senses. She couldn't think, didn't want to, no recourse, no options existing, other than submission.

He covered her mouth with his. The heat from him filled her, pouring into her, taking over her ability to do anything other than allow him free rein. She opened her mouth to him, offering all he would take, holding nothing back.

He tasted so damned good, like fresh mountain air, warming her, building need in her. She wanted him. All of him. Not just his kiss. Not just his hands in her hair. She needed him. Needed him to fill the void created from the time since she'd seen him last.

She dug her fingers into his jeans, working to take that thick cock in her hands. But the material prevented her, frustrating her, and she reached for the top button on his jeans.

The growl that emanated deep within him should have terrified her. His body vibrated from the intensity of it.

His mouth left hers, leaving her gasping, her lips already swollen, moisture coating them. She breathed in air that was his, filled with his scent, intoxicating her, making her feel wild, drunk with everything that was Rock.

His fingers combed through her hair, while his mouth tortured her jaw, lowering to her neck, nipping at the vulnerable spot at her nape.

"You are not listening to me, wild bitch." His throaty warning should have brought her pause.

"I can't help it." She arched into him, gripping the massive cock in his jeans. "You don't know how badly I need you."

He gripped her arms, squeezing her, confining her movement, pushing her from him. She could no longer feel his cock in her hand, and missed the heat from it immediately. She opened her eyes, a protest on her lips.

But he threw her. She became airborne, landing on the middle of his bed. The quickness of his action stunning her, exhilarating her, confusing her. Her hands dug into his comforter, her knees and feet pressing against the firmness of his mattress.

"You don't know what you are doing." His guttural tone made her wild.

He pounded his chest with his fist, glaring at her, his blond locks curling around his head, standing on end. His jaw had broadened, excitement and lust spawning the change in him. Teeth too long for a human pressed against his lips. His shirt stretched dangerously over muscles that were larger than they had been a moment before.

He towered over her, a beast and a man combined, large enough to terrify, to kill, to conquer.

"You are not strong enough to handle Cariboo." He beat his chest with his fist, his gaze almost appearing angry.

Her mouth went dry, and she ran her tongue over her lips. She would handle him. And he would not stop her. No matter the consequences. She would not turn back.

She kneeled on his bed, matching his glare, her heart pounding in her chest, her breath coming in pants. She pulled his T-shirt off of her, watching his gaze darken, his features harden, his hands drop to his sides, while he stared at her, naked on her knees in the middle of his bed.

"Don't tell me what I can and can't handle, wolf-man." Her voice didn't quaver, although she trembled from his dangerous appearance before her. She wouldn't fear him, couldn't cower from him, feeling deep in her gut that an intimidated bitch would turn him off.

He stalked her, moving to the bed with a grace impressive for a giant. His thick legs pressed into the softness of the blankets, altering the surface she kneeled upon.

"I will tell you what you can do, what you can't do, and when and how you shall do it." His words rumbled from him, chilling her blood, and sending fire to her core at the same time.

"No." Her body trembled even though she willed herself to remain confident before him. "If I am yours, then you are mine. And if I want you, then you shall give yourself to me, without holding back."

He grabbed her, the heat of his hand scalding her arm. Her knees scraped the bedspread, while he dragged her to him, lifting her up against him.

She reached for him, trying to grab at him, working to brace herself. But her efforts were for naught. He took her free hand and pinned it behind her. Her breasts pressed against the steel of his chest, muscles slightly altered, hard, large, crushing her.

The urge to fight him swam through her. He would like that, and sometime she might just do that. But right now, caution made her hesitate. He would dominate. She would allow that. But she would be satisfied too.

Before he could speak, she leaned into him, nipping his lower lip, tasting him, feeling moist heat saturate through her. Her insides churned, pressure building beyond her control. Her cum coated her pussy, its beautiful, musky scent surrounding them.

"You are so sure you can handle me being yours." His observation enticed her, made her want to prove to him how well she could handle him.

She had no doubts. Rock Toubec was everything she needed. And she would be all that he needed. If he wanted wild, she would give him wild. If he wanted aggression, she would meet his challenge.

He carried her, leaving the bed, making her blink with momentary confusion. And then he placed her in a chair. A plain chair, leaning against his wall. The chair left the ground, muscles rippling in his arms on either side of her as he lifted her, until she sat in the middle of his room.

"If you get up, I will spank you."

The dare was almost too much to resist. The sharp sting of a spanking could be so erotic. But he turned from her, leaving her, walking away from her to his closet. And she forgot to move, curiosity tingling through her, matching the rush of lust and desire that filled her.

He disappeared into the walk-in closet that she had browsed minutes before. Her heart pounded with an irregular beat, matching the pulse in her wrists and in her cunt. A rush of excitement brought on a cool sweat, her body tingling with electricity.

What was he doing in that closet?

Her ass pressed against the cool hardness of the wooden chair. Her bare feet were cushioned by the softness of the carpet underneath her. If she got up, went to see what kept him in that blasted closet, what would he do?

Impish exhilaration had her grinning. She curled her toes into the carpet, and pressed her hands against the side of the chair, ready to stand, prepared for the consequences, rushes of adrenaline making her pant.

And then he appeared. Crossing the room, he stood over her, one hand held out, a group of silk ties strung over his fingers.

"Today you will learn who is in charge."

Chapter Fifteen

Simone stared at the ties, an assortment of dark blues and blacks, thin and narrow, streaming over his hand. He let all but one of them slip from his hand, their soft touch gliding over her legs, falling to her feet.

"I don't understand." She leaned forward, but he blocked her, reaching over her, smothering her with muscle, with his rich male scent, with taut skin sprinkled with downy, reddish blond hair.

He grabbed her hand, pulling her arm behind her, behind the chair. Try as she would, she couldn't see, and didn't react soon enough to prevent her hands from being clasped together. One of his large hands pinned her wrists, her inner arms pressing against the side of the chair. The soft tie circled around her palms, her wrists, binding her, constricting her movement.

"Think you need to tie me down just to keep me in line?" She liked the idea, a smile tempting her lips.

He yanked on her wrists, tightening the knot, the soft material making movement of her hands impossible. Changing to her *lunewulf* form would break the bond, but in her flesh, she remained a captive.

She let her head drop, her hair fanning around her, limiting her view, allowing her to focus on the rise and fall of her breasts, her puckered nipples, her flat tummy, and her shaved pussy. She spread her legs, able to see pussy lips part, the smooth skin moist with her cum, her own desires carried in the air around her.

"Your confinement will allow you to learn." He spoke from behind her, but she saw no reason to turn and focus on his actions.

"And what do you want to teach me?"

She couldn't move her hands. She could stand, freeing herself of the chair, but her arms would remain confined, her wrists bound, her hands hanging against her ass.

Rock knelt next to her, picking up another tie. He leaned into her, brushing his cheek against hers, the roughness of his beard teasing her.

He kissed her neck, and then lowered his mouth to her breast. His teeth raked one nipple, then bit at the puckered flesh.

"Ouch. Oh. Shit." Gasping for air, she could hardly speak.

Pain shot through her, tortured pleasure filling her pussy with cream, making it throb, the rhythm matching that of her heart.

"Is that a complaint?"

It took a minute to catch her breath, his beautiful cobalt eyes watching her, waiting for her answer.

"No." Her answer came on an exhalation. Nothing he could do to her would make her complain. She was the focus of his attention, his touch, his taste. She couldn't think of a damned thing to complain about.

"Good girl." He took the second tie, and moved behind her.

The silky material grazed her arm. It took her a minute to realize he tied her arm to the back of the chair, confining her movement. She watched his actions as he picked up a third tie, and then tied her other arm to the other side. Now she and the chair were one. She wouldn't be able to stand without bringing the chair up with her.

"You're going to make me think you can't control me unless you tie me down." She watched him kneel next to her, grabbing a third tie.

"I can't teach you if you don't listen." He wrapped his large hand around her ankle, tying it to the leg of the chair.

With another tie, he bound her other foot. Now her arms and feet were one with the chair.

"And I am the only one who needs a lesson?" She loved the amused look he graced her with.

"Yes, little one. Today you will learn a very important lesson."

He hovered over her, kneeling, his eyes the most beautiful shade of sapphire, more relaxed than before, comfortable and confident. She had no doubt he could teach her many things. And she knew he would need to learn a few things as well. But for the moment, she would allow him his space, his need to control, to be in charge, to dominate her.

He ran rough fingertips over her forehead, around her eyes, across her cheeks, her mouth. She leaned into his touch, loving his petting, not wanting him to stop.

"So beautiful." His words caressed her. "So wild."

"I'm not the only one." She couldn't stay quiet. Whispering the words, she closed her eyes, feeling his hand stretch around her neck.

His long fingers wrapped around her neck, and she sucked in a long deep breath, knowing a werewolf could be killed if the neck were broken. Rock held her life in his hand, but she didn't fear him.

She had sensed before he needed to know she wouldn't be intimidated. Opening her eyes, she gazed at him through half-opened lids. He stroked her neck, stretching it, pushing under her jaw bone. His expression fogged with lust, desire, pure masculine pleasure of control intensifying his gaze.

"Your life is in my hands." He met her gaze, his fingers tightening ever so slightly around her neck.

"Yes." She understood this lesson. "I'm safe with you."

"I can protect you only if you obey me." The seriousness in his tone gave her pause, making her see how much he needed her loyalty.

She remembered the story of his previous mate being murdered, and wondered if the incident made him need her loyalty all the more.

"I will obey you." She met his gaze, knowing she had said the right thing when some of the darkness faded from those beautiful blue eyes. His grip relaxed. His hand glided down her front, cupping one of her breasts, squeezing, pulling. "Oh. Hell yes." Her eyes rolled into her head with pure delight, her toes curling into the carpet.

He grabbed both of her breasts, pulling them, kneading them, pinching her nipples.

She wanted to move, but bound to the chair she could do nothing. Arching into his touch, not wanting him to stop, her head fell back as a groan escaped her lips.

"Damn." She cried out, unprepared for the hot moisture of his mouth when he covered one of her nipples with his lips.

He suckled, tugged, twirled the puckered nub in his mouth. His teeth raked over her, shooting fiery currents straight to her toes. The roughness of his beard scraped over her skin, while his mouth soothed her with the steam of his lust.

Her pussy ached for attention, throbbed with need, craved to be stroked, fondled, fucked. She gyrated her hips on the chair, wanting him to focus his adoration on her cunt as well.

Rock tugged on her nipple until it popped free of his mouth, his teeth scraping over the sensitive skin.

"You are frustrated." Reddish blond hair stood on end around his flushed face. Dark blue eyes swam with amused passion.

"No. It feels good." She tugged on her restraints, wanting more than anything to touch him, caress the hardness of his body.

"Then why do you struggle?" He pulled on her breasts, her back arching toward him.

She groaned. "I want to touch you."

His laughter rumbled through him, while he continued to tug and knead her breasts. "And I told you this is not your day to play."

"Wolf-man." Her face was inches from his, their mixed scent intoxicating her with every breath. "You have played enough. Fuck me."

"You are giving the orders?" He let go of her breasts, leaving them reddened and tender from his attention.

"Only if you need help in giving them."

His fingers traced patterns down her abdomen, over her legs. And then he gripped her thighs, long fingers wrapping around her, lifting her ass off the chair, spreading her legs.

Rock's gaze lowered, focused on her pussy.

"You want that, don't you, wolf-man?" She would do anything to be able to lift her hips further, force her cunt into his face, make him suck the hot juices from her.

His growl tortured her. He wouldn't comment, wouldn't admit his craving to devour her. His actions, the intentness of his gaze, the tortured guttural sound ripping from his soul were answer enough. He craved her as much as she needed him.

His fingers crept along her skin, almost reaching her inflamed pussy, but not quite. He pressed into her, long powerful fingers pulling the tender flesh, opening her, exposing the humid folds.

"Tell me how badly you want me." She couldn't stand his silence, or his refusal to touch her pussy.

She thrust her hips toward his face, in spite of her silk bindings. The chair rocked underneath her, her leg muscles straining underneath his grip. She twisted her wrists against the ties, struggling now.

He didn't look up, ignoring her plight. His fingers pressed against the edge of her pussy. So close, but not close enough to soothe the fire in her cunt. Just one of those long, thick fingers could send her over the edge. If he would just thrust one finger deep into her cunt, she would come for him, for her. And damnit, she needed to come so badly.

"I can see your juices welling outside your pussy." His breath tickled her pussy, torturing her.

She let her head fall back, no longer able to watch his slow, torturous examination. Her eyes closed, and she groaned in frustration.

He pressed against her inner thighs, the imprint of his hand burning through her skin with its heat. Hands so powerful, fingers so thick and strong pushing her legs further apart.

She twisted her hands, the ties straining against her wrists. With all of her human strength, she fought to straighten her arms, loosen the binding that held her to the chair. What at first had excited her, now aggravated her, the desire to make him suck her cunt overwhelming her senses.

He ran a finger along the pulsing, inner folds of her pussy.

"Fuck yes." She bucked in the chair, the wood straining underneath her, but holding her annoyingly in place.

He backed away then. Standing, his presence towered over her. She lifted her head, her vision hesitating a moment before clearing, enabling her to see the giant god who stood over her, hooded lids half-covering the smoldering gaze he gave her.

"What are you doing?" She wanted his hands back on her, his attention focused on her body, her needs.

Instead he turned away from her, walking to the other side of the room, buns of steel visible through his jeans, thick leg muscles straining the denim with his slow movements.

His back remained to her while he pulled his T-shirt from his body, shoulder and back muscles making her mouth wet. She yanked at her ties, working to pull her wrists apart from each other, fighting to straighten her legs.

"Be careful. The chair could fall over." He turned to face her, making her breath catch in her throat at the magnificence of his bare chest, muscles rippling under tanned skin, chest hair curling across well-defined pectorals.

Daylight did wonders for Rock's good looks. Dark and brooding. Magnificent and powerful. Confident and patient. Too damned fucking patient.

He reached for the top button of his jeans, making heat wash over her. She no longer tried to free herself, but kept her gaze locked on his hand, slowly unbuttoning that top button of his jeans.

"You need to learn to be careful what you want." His voice was guttural, barely above a whisper.

If she didn't know better, she would think he threatened her. She chanced a glance at his face, and noticed immediately the silver hue to his blue eyes. His beast threatened him, the realization making her want to tear free of her bondage.

He unzipped his pants, then stripped before her, until he stood naked, his cock jutting forward. She gave up trying to slow her breathing, unable to take her attention from the thickness, the length, the perfection of the cock in front of her. Her breath came in pants, her mouth too dry, and then too moist.

"This is what you do to me." He moved close. So close. But she couldn't reach for him, couldn't touch him, couldn't taste him.

"Let me show you what you do to me." Simone could hardly speak.

His cock was right there. Right in front of her.

"I know what I'm doing to you." He moved around her, circling her, that giant cock taunting her with its nearness.

"This isn't fair. You have made your point already." She yanked at her ties, needing his cock, craving to touch him, wanting more than anything to give both of them pleasure.

"Have I?" He moved further away from her, and she had to strain her neck to see he had walked over toward the window, his back to her. "Do you understand that fucking you will make you mine? This won't be casual sex. Not for you and me. Do you hear what I am saying?"

"I am already yours, Rock." She allowed her muscles to alter, just a bit, feeling the ties strain as she tugged her wrists apart. "Let me show you how much I want to be yours."

"I know how much you want to fuck, little one." He clasped his hands behind his back, continuing to face the window.

Why wouldn't he turn around and face her?

He would not send her away a second time frustrated and empty. Damnit to hell and back, he would give her what they both wanted.

The chair cracked, while fibers in the tie began to snap. Her hearing fine-tuned to every sound while muscles inside her altered their shape from human to *lunewulf.* Bones in her spine popped, making the position on the chair uncomfortable. The ties ripped, her confinement ceasing, while her body transformed, smooth white fur covered her skin, and teeth grew in her mouth while her jaw altered its shape.

Rock turned, his anger leaping forward, filling the room with its spicy pungency, so strong she almost sneezed.

"Already you disobey me?" He leapt forward, metamorphosis consuming him while he approached her.

She shoved the chair out of the way, leaping toward him.

You will not ignore me! Her growl rumbled through her.

Half man, half Cariboo *lunewulf*, he grew with such intensity before her that the room suddenly seemed too small.

He swatted at her, striking her in midair, his arm slamming against the side of her body, knocking the wind from her, throwing her off balance.

Don't you understand? Her bark got knocked out of her as she hit the floor. *Don't keep me away from you.*

Her bones altered faster than normal, emotions rushing through her. Why did this wolf have to be so damned confusing? He was powerful, strong, with goals and drive. Nothing about him was lacking. She couldn't have created a more perfect mate if she had tried. And she wouldn't allow something like male ego, his need to see her submit, prevent her from having him.

She scurried to her feet, ready to take him on. "I don't like being ignored." Her legs trembled, but she tried to show her assuredness, gripping her waist with her hands, and glaring at him.

His human form didn't return as quickly. Silver streamed through sapphire eyes that flashed with anger and lust. His broad chest heaved in and out, a warrior ready to take down his victim. But his cock. That massive cock remained on full alert, ready to impale her, eager to claim her for his own.

"Ignored?" He uttered the word as if not understanding.

She didn't have time to react, wasn't ready for his quick movement. For such a huge man, he did his lineage justice with his speed. He grabbed her arm, his hand smoldering as long fingers trapped her, lifted her, held on to her until she landed on her belly on his bed.

"You don't wish to be ignored?" He was on her before she could move.

Chapter Sixteen

Simone sprawled on his bed, her adorable round ass staring up at him. The smoothness of her legs wreaked havoc on his already tortured senses as they brushed against his thighs. He gripped her hips, feeling her silky skin.

Her ass spread, cum dripping from her pussy, her sexual cravings filling the air around him, making it impossible to think straight. He had never met a more obstinate, willful, wild bitch. She was so fucking sexy, so damned hot, and in need of a firm hand for her own good.

A bitch like this would take up his time, consume his thoughts, make his life pure hell. He had told himself over the past few years that he wouldn't seek out a mate, not after what happened to Dana. And if an appealing bitch happened to come along, she would have to be docile, already tame, not in need of continual supervision.

So what the fuck had happened?

Simone tossed her blonde hair to the side, looking over her shoulder. She tried to push herself to her hands and knees, ready to take him on. He couldn't believe she actually challenged him. Didn't she realize she was half his size? But the little white werewolf had actually leapt through the air, ready to pounce on him.

Thinking of her attacking him, demanding he fuck her, scalded his rational thought, drove need through him like molten lava. His cock throbbed, fire burning through his blood, the heat of it consuming him, making it impossible to think of anything other than that hot little cunt.

She arched her ass, making the view more enticing.

"Tell me you haven't forgotten how." She mocked him.

How dare the little bitch try to take the upper hand with him.

"You are out of line, my little one." He pulled her toward him, making her slide along the bed, lifting her pussy to his cock

The moist heat made his penis buck, eager to dive deep into that beautiful pussy. He pressed against her, his cock head immediately soaked with her thick cream.

"Dear God. You are so fucking hot." His cock swelled with anticipation, a rush of Cariboo adrenaline tearing through him.

He could be wild, aggressive, even violent if he allowed his cravings to release. She made it so fucking hard to maintain control. And he knew she had no idea what she did to him, how her teasing and her challenges ripped through to the soul of the beast within him. He didn't want to hurt her, had no desire to scare her, but she pushed harder than she should.

Her muscles stretched, humidity soaring around his cock, burning his flesh, shredding his ability to think straight. His cock sunk into her cunt, her hole opening, her hot fluids flowing around him.

How long had it been since he had fucked a woman? He couldn't remember. But he had never been with a bitch who was so tight, so fucking hot, and felt so damned good to sink into.

"Damn. Oh God. Fuck. Are you going to fit?" Her cries gave him energy, encouraged his plunge.

Her hands balled into fists. Silky blonde hair fanning around her as she shook her head from one side to the other. She arched, allowing him to sink even deeper into her cunt.

"Oh yes. I'm going to fit. You are going to take all of me." His shaft disappeared into her pussy, and his balls brushed against her smooth skin.

For good measure, he thrust forward, watching while she gripped the bedspread with her fists.

Her moist pussy tightened around him. He retreated slowly, enjoying how her muscles clung to his cock, seeing her cream spread over his skin. Her cum eased his path, but before he was halfway out he had to feel her heat again. He sunk deep inside her, watching her body arch and tighten, ready for him this time.

The heat of her pussy matched the temperature of his body. Feverish desire to plunge into her, again and again, overwhelmed him. He could no longer sustain slow movement. His cock swelled but he wouldn't end their lovemaking yet.

She was so slick, so smooth, her fiery moisture aiding his journey. He picked up the pace, gripping her hips. His cock buried deep within her burning abyss, then he pulled out, feeling the lack of heat, then plunged again. Faster. Harder.

His eyes rolled into his head, darkness allowing him to feel the pleasures this perfect, little *lunewulf* bitch offered him. She was so tight, and the more he thrust, it seemed the more her muscles clamped around him. He could fuck her forever.

He leaned into her, sliding his hands over her back. The scent of her cum, the dampness of her skin, the quickness of her breath, filled the air around him, heightening his senses. Blood pumped through him at a furious rate, making his heart pound, and sweat pearl over his skin.

Bent over her like this, he could reach a new depth in her creamy warmth. Moisture spilled around his balls, making them tighten. They slapped her clit every time he impaled her, the smoothness of her skin teasing the fragile sacks.

"That is so fucking good." She panted her words, gasping every time he thrust.

But he wanted to give her more than just good. This wouldn't be a one-time fuck. No other werewolf would ever be able to handle Simone—not that pack leader, not any of them. He would brand her with his cock, explode inside her, locking her to him. When he was done, she would know to whom she belonged.

He lunged into her, her pussy smooth and hot, gripping and releasing while he fucked her with all that he had.

"You're going to scream." He pounded her cunt with his cock. "You're going to come like you've never come before. And when you do, you're going to scream my name."

She grunted. More like howled. Her sound so raw, letting him know he fucked her thoroughly enough that she could no longer speak.

Fire built between the two of them, his cock burning with the need to explode. Muscles strained throughout him. He fought to keep his beast at bay, not wanting to hurt her, knowing she wasn't ready for such carnal sex.

"Rock." Her pussy muscles started to spasm around his cock. "Rock!" She cried out again, "Rock!"

Her pussy grew so tight he could hardly move, the inner muscles collapsing around his shaft. But then her orgasm caused fiery heat to lubricate her cunt.

Simone couldn't breathe. Rock impaled her with a cock larger than anything she had ever experienced. Every time he moved inside her, torrents of pleasure blazed through her. It was as if he fucked her entire body, and not just her cunt.

When air finally filled her lungs, she felt almost lightheaded. She swooned, almost collapsing but not wanting to miss a stroke of his cock.

"Don't stop. Please. Don't stop." If he could make her come again, like he just did, she wasn't sure she would live through it. But she sure as hell wanted to see if she could.

The mattress caved under her, giving her the sensation of sliding backwards. Rock pressed his knees into the bed. Strong fingers glided through her hair, gripping it, pulling her up.

"Do you think you can handle more?" He pressed her backside to him, the moistness of their skin mixing.

"I can handle all you can dish out." She wasn't at all sure that was the case, but she knew she wouldn't cry out first.

His laugh vibrated against her back, making his cock buck inside her. Pressure began slowly, another orgasm building.

"Better be careful, my sweet little one." His breath tickled her ear, sending chills racing over her skin. "I think you know that you can't keep up with me."

Oh! The pompous ass! She would show him.

She twisted in his arms, the moist sheen of their bodies easing her movement. His grip tightened, but she managed to slide her pussy off of his cock.

"You don't think I can keep up with you?" She met his gaze, dark sapphires glistening with silver stared down at her.

Body sweat and cum lingered between them. Hands so strong they could crush her, glided up her arms, and then gripped her shoulders. Rational thought failed her momentarily. She was so awestruck by the intensity of him.

"You can't." A grin tempted his lips, his amusement all too clear. "You are fragile and small."

She shoved him to the side, allowing just a bit of muscle to grow within her in order to aid her plight. There was no way she could push him backwards, or release his grip on her. He might be the stronger creature, but he wouldn't see her as less of an equal. His line of thinking needed adjusting immediately.

"I'll show you who is fragile and small." She caught him off guard, but more than likely he didn't fight her.

She brought him down on to the bed, and straddled him before he could get up. He might be the stronger, but she knew how to immobilize a man. His cock was like a velvet rod of steel. She wrapped her fingers around it, placing it at the entrance of her pussy.

He stretched out underneath her, propping his hands behind his head, and appeared more comfortable and smug than she cared to see him. Her actions hadn't convinced him that she could handle him, only that she was up to the challenge. His long legs stretched out behind her, forcing her to keep her balance so she wouldn't fall off of him while he adjusted himself.

"Do what you will, my little one. I won't stop you."

Of that, she had no doubts.

He was so thick that her fingers barely wrapped around the shaft of his cock. She positioned his cock head at her entrance, feeling the pressure as she slid down on to him.

He impaled her. That mighty cock gutted her cunt, filling her, stretching her, until she thought he would force his way in up to her bellybutton. Sparks flew in front of her, her breath swept from her lungs. The power of his cock surged through her, until she couldn't think straight.

But she had to think. She had to maintain control. She would bring him to his climax. She would make him come. That would be the only way he would see her as strong, and not some weak, frail woman, who needed to be guided and protected.

"When you come, you will scream *my* name." She began riding his cock, moving up and down slowly, his hands gripping her hips. "Do you understand me, wolf-man?"

His grin about made her lose it. He was so damned sexy. Blue eyes sparkled with amusement, and the way his blond hair fell around his face added to his macho appearance.

"Yes, ma'am." His drawl was like honey.

She grabbed his wrists when he tried to force her down on his cock. "Give me your hands." She couldn't force him to do anything, but he seemed willing to cooperate, which was all she could hope for.

He released her hips, and she guided him by the wrists until his hands rested on either side of his face. Pinning him like this forced her to stretch over his thick torso, while maintaining the slow ride that tortured her worse than him, she feared.

She raised up on her legs, her inner thighs stretching over him, and then sank down on his cock, burying him deep inside her. He filled her like no werewolf ever had, brushing against inner muscles that had never been tormented so wonderfully before. She pushed off of him again, then eased back down, enjoying the pure pleasure of his cock.

He didn't fight her, but let her have her fun. His hands relaxed underneath her grip. And she rode his cock, aware of the heat consuming her, the muscles tightening, the orgasm building like a tidal wave and she knew she would explode soon.

"Fuck me, baby. Damn, you are so hot." His words vibrated through his chest, the baritone caressing her senses.

He leaned forward, sucking in one of her nipples. Tingles shot through her, exploding like mini-fireworks throughout her. She was on the verge of exploding, and didn't want to come before he did.

"You aren't playing fair," she cried out.

His teeth raked over the puckered flesh, and then he bit, sending quick electric charges straight to her cunt.

"Damn you." She couldn't hold back any longer.

She pressed her legs into the bed, raising her pussy until his cock barely entered her. Then she slammed down on him, wanting him to fill her, needing to break the dam.

He suckled her breast like a starving child, filling his mouth with her. She couldn't raise herself, without breaking the suction he'd created. All she could do was ride him, moving her hips as fast as she could go. The heat consumed her, fire burning that she fanned by pounding her pussy up and down on his cock.

Rock released her breast, and his expression grew brutal, determination spilling out in his gaze. "Damnit. Simone!"

"Come inside me." She thrust her cunt down on his shaft, filling and releasing, molten flames roaring through her.

Those dark sapphire eyes hardened, his mouth forming a straight line. She had him. She forced him deep inside her, holding his wrists, feeling his arm muscles contort under her grasp. His legs straightened, the length of him underneath her as hard as a board.

"Dear God. Woman. Little bitch!" He closed his eyes. Control contorting his expression.

The swelling inside her peaked, no longer could she hold back the rush of desire that fucking him had created. The spasms started deep inside her womb, building, intensifying. She crashed down on his cock, gripping his hips with her inner thigh muscles. Wave after wave rushed through her. Everything around her seemed to start in a slow spin. Her orgasm fogged her senses, blurring her vision, muting all sound. Her world became a rush of simmering cum, her pussy filling, coating his cock, dripping out of her.

Rock pushed his arms forward, but grabbed her before she could slip to the side. Her world altered, her orgasm still drifting through her. He moved her, his arms circling around her while he moved into a sitting position, pressing his cock deep into the tenderest part of her cunt.

His cock swelled. Hot semen filling her as he came deep inside her.

"Simone!" His growl exploded through him. Her name vibrating through her. "Mine," he howled. "Simone! You are mine!"

Chapter Seventeen

Reality hit harder than a ton of bricks. Rock had just mated with her. The age-old tradition of werewolves, claiming a bitch through sexual intercourse, was still taken quite seriously in most packs. And she knew Rock meant that she was his permanently.

She should feel ecstatic. This was what she wanted. Rock Toubec would be a challenge, but she could tame the beast in him, she knew she could. But she couldn't deny the overwhelming fear that gripped her with his words.

"Rock." She could hardly utter his name, her mouth suddenly too dry.

His cock still filled her, the heat of him making it hard to find the words she needed to say.

Rock leaned back on his bed, pulling her down with him. The warmth of his body clung to her, his powerful arms wrapping around her. She should feel secure, wonderfully content and sated. But nerves tortured her, anticipating his reaction to her news. Her insides twisted in knots.

"There is something you don't know." The urge to pull away from him crept through her.

"Tell me anything you want." He sounded very relaxed, although his hold on her was firm. "Why are you suddenly nervous?"

She should have realized her emotions would be strong enough to alert him.

Best to get it over with. "I don't think we can be mated yet."

He rolled to his side, his cock gliding out of her pussy, leaving her empty, the comfort of him inside her gone. Fiery moisture flowed from her cunt, the extreme humidity saturating her legs. He cuddled her next to him, looking down at her. His fingers traced lines down the side of her face, brushing her hair to the side. Sultry eyes, desire still glazing his expression, grazed over her slowly.

"We are mated." The finality of his words sunk through her like an anchor.

She attempted a smile but her lips quivered. Would he understand the ridiculous pack law that bound her to three other werewolves?

She cleared her throat and sat up, the sudden movement making her dizzy.

"There is a slight complication." When she met his gaze she saw the contented look slowly fading.

He narrowed his gaze on her, and she slid off the edge of the bed. Her legs were like jelly.

"And what is this complication?" Rock stood as well, and then walked around the bed, approaching her slowly.

Unleashed power gleamed off of him. Completely naked, with a body that should be outlawed, he moved in on her. The man messed with her equilibrium, making her thoughts steer toward fucking him again.

She lowered her gaze, unable to look at him and keep her thoughts focused. And this was important.

"Grandmother Rousseau passed a law before she died. You might have heard of it. She assigned three mates to every bitch in the pack." Maybe it was best to say it fast, get it out quickly and pray he would understand.

"I'm aware of the law." He walked to her side of the bed, narrowing the distance between them, then brushing his fingers across her cheek, tangling his hand in her hair. "That law doesn't affect us."

"Actually it does." She sucked in a breath of air, wishing she had something to drink. "That werewolf in Howley's who was bothering me was one of my assigned mates."

"Have you fucked him?"

"No. God. No. I haven't fucked any of them." She walked around him, gratified that he didn't hold her. She needed air to breathe that didn't have their sex clinging to it. If her head was clear she could make him understand. "I left the pack shortly after the law was passed. This is the first time I've been back, and one of my assigned mates just happened to find me."

She turned, wanting his reaction. The hard, muscular curve of his ass distracted her. Her pussy throbbed, heat searing her from the inside out. He turned to face her, a warrior's body, hard and powerful. Nerves tingled through her with the penetrating stare he gave her, those deep blue eyes burrowing straight to her soul.

"You are today, and shall be until the day you die, Simone Toubec."

Her heart skipped a beat. Simone Toubec. She liked the sound of that.

He relaxed his stance, and the air around her seemed to relax as well. A slow smile crept over his lips, making her wonder if he realized the appeal of her new name as well.

"You won't worry about this anymore." He approached her, his gait easy and relaxed.

She wished she could say the same about her insides. His cock remained semi-hard, her cum covering it, teasing her with the rich smell. Muscles rippled as he moved in on her, wrapping her in his arms, then tenderly kissing her forehead.

"I want you to bring your cub over so we may all have supper together." His lips brushed over her face, and then down the side of her neck. "I shall tend to this issue of that ridiculous law later."

* * * * *

Johann didn't like the werewolf. Armand Gaston stood in his living room, watching Samantha, who lounged on the couch. Johann couldn't help but think the man looked more like he would change into a bulldog than a wolf if he morphed. Armand had his hands on his hips, arguing his point concerning Simone.

"What of her other two mates?" Samantha stood with incredible ease, considering her growing tummy. "I mean, if you are claiming Simone based on this law, shouldn't all three of you be claiming her together?"

Johann fought a grin over the defiant sparkle he saw in his mate's eyes. Not to mention, her quick thinking made her invaluable. He turned his attention to Armand, who seemed to be groping for an answer.

"I haven't sought out her other mates," the stocky man said finally. "If they wish to stake their claim, that is their right by law."

"I've had numerous complaints about this law." Johann didn't see any harm in letting the werewolf know his thinking on the matter. "We aren't a democracy, but I will allow discussion of it at the next meeting."

Dissolving the law seemed the best solution. He certainly wouldn't require any further mating to take place under the law. But the existing tetrads would require a bit of delicacy in dissolving. Not all of them had been unsuccessful. And there was the issue of who would end up with whom. The whole matter was a blasted mess.

"Are you saying then that you will not honor a current law on the books?" Armand squinted his beady, pale eyes, the thick folds of skin around them making them almost disappear.

"Hardly." This short brute wouldn't corner him. "But as my mate just pointed out, the law states the females have three werewolves as mates, and you are just one. Come to the next pack meeting, and we will discuss it further then."

"Well, I do know one thing." Armand turned toward the front door, and not soon enough. Johann would much rather be enjoying time alone with Samantha while Jere slept, than listening to this werewolf whine. Armand held on to the doorknob, but turned and pointed a finger at him. "I do know that Rock Toubec is not one of Simone's mates by law."

"What does he have to do with any of this?" Johann hid the trickle of trepidation that slithered through him at the mention of the Cariboo *lunewulf*.

"He is the one who pulled her away from me earlier." Armand stuck out his pudgy chin, or what there was of it. "God only knows where he hauled her off to."

"I'll look into the matter." Johann had a very good idea where Toubec would have taken Simone, and he doubted the bitch fought him off in the slightest.

"You do that." Armand turned and left, the door closing behind him.

"And how exactly do you plan on looking into the matter?"

He turned around to see Samantha standing there with her hands on her hips, looking too damned sexy, even with her brown eyes challenging him.

"This is part of being pack leader." He reached for her but she grabbed his hand, squeezing his fingers.

"Could you make some phone calls?" She pulled his hand to her mouth, nipping at the flesh by his knuckle.

He could use the pack directory, learn the number out to Toubec's ranch. But if Simone were in danger, he wouldn't be able to tell over the phone. Samantha's pouty expression turned contemplative. He could tell she contemplated the same thing.

"I'm not trying to control her life." He brushed a reassuring kiss across her forehead. "But if Simone is after this werewolf, she won't stop to notice if he is safe or not."

"Is that how she was with you?" Samantha's brown eyes looked up at him with curiosity, and worry. "Did she chase you without thinking?"

"That was a long time ago." He ran his hands over her cropped blonde hair, holding her head in place so she would look at him. Her gaze never left his face. "To be fair, I chased her a bit too. But Samantha. You are my mate. And I don't regret that for a day."

He could see her hesitation, could tell she wanted to believe him but wasn't sure that she could. And he understood her doubts. She thought they had mated because she carried his cub. But the bitch was so full of life, so beautiful, so quick-witted, she had to know how much he loved her. Every day he realized the catch he had in her, but he knew only his actions would help her to see that.

"If you can prove Rock isn't a murderer, would you approve Simone mating with him?"

"I've got to get rid of that blasted law first." Johann could see how she hoped to pin his true feelings with her question. He smiled, needing her to see his interest in Simone was simply for her wellbeing. "But if the Cariboo *lunewulf* makes her happy, then I would agree to the mating."

"Well then, we need to figure out who killed those women, because I really think Simone has fallen for him." Samantha pushed away from him, and he enjoyed the sway of her ass when she walked into the kitchen. "Go make sure she is safe. But don't piss her off, Johann. She can't stand confinement anymore than you or I can."

* * * * *

Johann had been to this ranch many times growing up when the Rousseaus still owned it. And for the most part, it looked the same. He imagined some hard feelings still harbored from Toubec being the new owner.

The Suburban popped over the gravel in the drive as he came to a stop, and took a minute to gaze across the plush meadows that spread out around the large home. Toubec had got himself quite a deal with this place. The land was healthy, and could be used for timber as well as ranching.

He wandered toward the house, but a noise distracted him, and he turned to see two cubs in fur come racing toward him. By the size of them, he would have guessed them to be in their teens, but their actions were more those of young cubs.

Teeth bared and nipping at each other, they tumbled around the side of the house, but came up short when they saw him standing there. He remembered seeing the two boys with Toubec the first night he met him after the funeral. More than likely, these two rambunctious balls of fur were his cubs. He envied the privacy the ranch offered, allowing them to run in their fur in the sunshine.

"Where is your father?" He looked from one young werewolf to the other.

One of them snarled at him, and then turned to dart around the side of the house. The other one bit his tail, and the two of them rolled over each other in the gravel drive.

Another werewolf appeared around the side of the house, an older bitch, and by the size of her, a Cariboo *lunewulf.* She barked furiously at the cubs, until they separated.

"Excuse me, ma'am." Johann turned around, putting his back to the three of them, offering the older woman privacy to change into her human form and don her clothes so he could speak to her.

"What can I do for you?" The older woman walked past him toward the house, adjusting her sweatshirt, toward the house.

She was tall, almost as tall as he was, and a stout woman, possibly in her fifties. He wondered if she might be Toubec's mother.

"I'm here to check up on a single bitch who might be out here." He followed her to the house, the two boys, both naked, darting past them. "I don't think we've met yet. I'm Johann Rousseau."

He held his hand to shake hers but she ignored it.

"You might be too late." She grinned at him, her right eye tooth missing.

"What do you mean by that?" He nodded his thanks to her when she held the door open for him, allowing him to enter the living room he had been in many times as a youth.

"I mean she might not be a single bitch anymore." The woman elbowed him in the side, which hurt, and then chuckled at her own joke. "Rock brought me her clothes a while back to wash up for him."

"Why would he bring you her clothes?" Johann glanced around the house, trying to remember its layout. "Where are they now?"

"I guess they were dirty." She kept walking while she talked, and led him into the kitchen. "And before we left they were upstairs."

One of the cubs appeared wearing shorts, which were twisted at his waist. "Where's Daddy? I want to see that new mommy he brought."

The other cub appeared behind his brother, and hit the boy in the head. "He isn't bringing a new mommy. You don't know anything."

"Your father isn't upstairs?" Johann turned to face the two boys.

They were almost the same size, one just a few inches taller than the other. Both had curly blond hair, and a face full of freckles.

"Nope." The shorter of the two answered, not looking at Johann, but instead headed for the refrigerator.

"Nate, you stay out of the food." She intercepted the child, who scowled, and turned toward the back door. The large bitch wagged a finger at both of them. "Nate. Hunter. You make sure your chores are done before I call you in for supper."

"Let's go find daddy," Johann heard one of them say before the two cubs darted out the back door.

"Guess they aren't here." She shrugged, offering no other conversation, but instead started humming while rummaging through the refrigerator she had just prevented the boys from opening.

"I noticed his truck parked out front." Johann watched her pull out containers, and place them on the counter. "Do you mind if I take a look around?"

Turning, the large woman's watery blue eyes gazed at him for a moment. She pursed her lips, summing him up. Johann offered one of his irresistible smiles.

"I'm being forward. Forgive me." He had used less charm on many women in the past, with much success. "I should have mentioned I'm the new pack leader." He grinned, nodding toward the door. "From the looks of it, you keep pretty busy around here. I'm sure that's why we haven't met yet."

The stout woman blushed, running her chubby fingers through whitish, blonde hair cropped at the shoulders. Dimples spread over her broad cheeks when she smiled, and although far from a handsome bitch, he could see amusement sparkle in her eyes.

"I'm Quinette. But you call me Quinnie just like everyone else does." She gripped both of his hands in a crushing handshake, then turned away quickly, returning to her task.

"It's a pleasure to meet you, Quinnie." He edged toward the back door, hoping she wouldn't offer resistance to him searching out her boss. "If you don't mind, I'll follow the cubs and see if they can lead me to their father."

"Help yourself." She faced him, holding a large onion in one hand, and a sharp knife in the other. "You know. He might have taken that little bitch out to see the cabins. Rock has a weakness for those old rundown buildings."

She turned, and whacked the onion in half, with one swift movement. He watched half of the onion topple to the side on the counter, its fresh pungency filling the air.

He mumbled his thanks, and then left out the back door the boys had used to escape moments ago.

* * * * *

He shouldn't just be wandering the man's property. Johann knew he pushed his rights as pack leader just a bit. But here was an opportunity to take a good look at the ranch, and see what there was to see. So far, it looked like a well-run ranch.

And what exactly did he expect to find? He wasn't a detective, and had no idea what to look for to determine if a person was a murderer or not.

A couple of ranch hands, one of whom he went to high school with, noticed his trek across the open meadow. They said something to each other, then sheltered their eyes with their hands to take another look at him. He offered a wave, deciding to appear confident in his mission. They waved back, then disappeared around one of the outbuildings.

If Toubec was in the area, he would learn of Johann's presence soon enough. The row of forgotten cabins appeared beyond the trees. Murder shrouded what otherwise would be a wonderful sanctuary. He stopped, sniffing the air, determining that there were no werewolves in the area.

Well, the wolf hadn't brought Simone out here. The best thing to do would be to head back. Simone's safety was his top priority at the moment. Something grabbed his attention though, something faint, lingering in the air. An uncomfortable feeling pitted in his stomach, encouraging him forward, instead of turning back.

"Holy shit." Johann covered his nose from the stench, his human form not able to hinder his heightened senses and stared into the group of trees.

There, hanging from one of the branches, was a naked woman, her head bent at an odd angle, long blonde hair covering her face.

Chapter Eighteen

A twinge of excitement tingled in Simone's stomach when they pulled off the highway, onto the long winding gravel road leading to Rock's home. Jere sat seat-belted between Simone and Rock, her bright, curious eyes staring toward the sprawling ranch house. Rock rested his arm along the top of the seat behind them, his fingers caressing Simone's shoulder.

"Here we are." Rock focused on Jere, who still wouldn't look at him.

Simone studied his profile. His strong jawline, with his close shaven beard and high cheekbones, made him appear regal. Biceps bulged through his shirt sleeve. His large, strong hands rested easily on the steering wheel, hands that could fondle and caress her. Those hands could also grip her breasts, squeezing them, torture them until she came. Her nipples puckered into hard beads at the thought.

She wouldn't pinch herself to see if she were dreaming. Rock Toubec was a leader among werewolves, a man to be reckoned with, and he was hers. When he looked her way, Simone saw the smoldering desire in those dark blue orbs that matched the craving building inside her, making her pussy throb.

"What do we have here?" He had turned his attention from her, focusing on the road.

The Suburban sat parked in front of his house. Samantha had told them Johann had come out here to check up on her, so Simone wasn't surprised to see it. But a knot formed in her gut at the sight of a police car, and another, dark blue car, the same make as the cop car, with city tags, also parked in front of Rock's home.

Rock parked, then jumped out of the truck, slamming the door before she could get Jere out of her seatbelt.

She pulled her thoughts together, focusing on her daughter, and then Rock, who glanced around the yard before turning toward the house.

"What could be wrong?" Simone hopped out of the truck, then helped her daughter out.

Jere refused to walk, so Simone carried her inside, following Rock. She hoped her daughter would relax some, although she remembered the last encounter Jere had with Rock's cubs. It would take a while for the three children to get accustomed to each other. Werewolf cubs were known to fight until they got used to each other.

"We got trouble." Hanson stood in the middle of the living room, anger surrounding him.

Rock tensed next to her, his powerful muscles seeming to grow, stretching his shirt. The sultry gaze he'd worn all the way out here disappeared, and his expression became all business.

"What kind of trouble?" Rock ran his hand through his hair, his attention focused hard on his ranch manager.

"That pack leader found a bitch hung in one of the trees over by the cabins." Hanson glanced her way, giving her the impression he wished she wasn't in the room.

"How did Johann find a dead body?" Simone didn't understand. Why would he be out on Rock's land?

Hanson pointed toward the kitchen. He didn't look at her, but continued to talk to Rock. "Quinnie in there told the pack leader he could wander around looking for you."

Quinnie appeared from the dining room, possibly hearing her name mentioned and feeling a need to defend her actions. She wiped her chubby hands on her apron. One of Rock's cubs walked around her, watching the men.

Jere squirmed in her arms at the sight of the boy.

"Where is the pack leader now? And where are the cops?" Rock headed toward the hallway, with Hanson on his heels.

"Apparently Rousseau called the cops. I sure didn't. But they are all out where the body is. I headed back here when one of the hands spotted your truck on the road." Hanson followed Rock.

The two men entered a room that looked like an office. She stood in the doorway, Jere straining in her arms to see over her shoulder, more than likely keeping an eye on Rock's cubs.

Muscles quivered in her arms after her daughter pushed to be free. She leaned against the doorway, feeling anything but calm. Rock, on the other hand, appeared completely in control. So tall, with broad shoulders, and chest muscles rippling under his shirt. She could stare at him all day, knowing all would be okay with him to handle matters.

He grabbed a cell phone from its charger, clipped it to his belt, and then turned toward her, Hanson on his heels. The heat of his hand warmed the back of her head. His fingers wrapped through her hair, wrapping around the back of her neck.

Why the hell did something like this have to happen again? More than anything, she wanted him to stay by her side, touching her, spending time with her.

"Quinnie. Lock all the doors and windows when we leave." He still held her neck when they reached the kitchen. "I'm taking my cell, so you can call me if needed."

Quinnie nodded, then grabbed one of Rock's cubs when he looked like he was going to jump on Jere.

The last thing Simone wanted was to be locked in his house while he was out chasing down bad guys. This wasn't her idea of how they would be mated. She wouldn't be put on a shelf, taken down only when things were safe and calm.

"You will not leave this house." Rock had turned to her, rubbing his fingers up her neck to her cheek.

She could swear he read her thoughts. When she would have spoken her mind, he lowered his mouth to hers. His kiss was passionate, mind-boggling, ripping all thought of arguing from her. He covered her mouth, his tongue swirling around hers, while he pulled her to him, crushing her against his steel chest.

She about lost her balance and grabbed his shirt, balling the material with her fists, just to hold on. He leaned her back, bending over her, devouring her mouth, the heat from his mouth capturing her senses, making her forget where she was.

Who cared that they had an audience? She returned his kiss, ravishing his mouth, craving the taste of him. Liquid fire raced through her, while her pussy swelled and began throbbing. He left her gasping, her lips tingling and feeling almost bruised, when he lifted his head. Dark blue eyes held her attention, and she couldn't look away from him.

"Keep your ass in this house." He whispered his command, but that didn't undermine the authority in his words. "If you disobey me, I swear I will tan your hide."

He walked out the back door, not waiting to see if she had a response. The best thing to do would be to confront him later about being bossy and possessive. She had her work cut out for her in taming this wolf.

* * * * *

The look of defiance Simone gave him before he left made Rock nervous. How could he protect her if she took off running, trying to take matters into her own hands? It crossed his mind to leave Hanson at the house to guard the place. But the old wolf would growl and throw a bloody fit if he kept him out of the action. Hopefully it wouldn't take too long dealing with the cops. He had his doubts however.

"Where have you been?" Toby Beuerlein walked toward him when Rock entered his coveted sanctuary area.

How dare someone take the only sacred part of this ranch, and defile it with murder. He noticed the naked, blonde bitch immediately, her skin already appearing gray. Death clung to the air, filling his nostrils, making him want to gag, to strike out, to do serious damage to whoever had managed to pull this off.

Beuerlein stared at him, waiting for an answer, but the detective could just wait. Where he had been, and what he had been doing, had nothing to do with this death.

"I thought we had wolves patrolling the area?" He took his anger out on his ranch manager. "How the hell did this happen?"

"This one hasn't been dead long." Matthew Jordeaux, the pack doctor, joined them, clear plastic gloves on his hands. "This isn't official yet, but I would say her neck was broken just a few hours ago."

A few hours ago he was fucking Simone in his bedroom! Rock could hardly suppress the rage that swarmed through him.

"Where is Johann Rousseau?" Rock glanced at the two werewolves cutting the rope, bringing the body to the ground. "I heard he found her."

"He called me." Beuerlein kept an eagle eye on him. Rock felt his irritation growing right along with his rage. "Apparently right after he noticed the bitch hanging in the tree, he heard someone and took off after them."

"He saw who did this?" Rock gave the detective his full attention. "Who the hell was it?"

"I haven't been able to reach him since his initial call." Beuerlein turned, squinting toward the thick evergreens that offered privacy to the cabins. "I sent a couple of werewolves out to see if they could track him down."

But since he was pack leader, Rock knew they wouldn't take Johann down. They would seek him out, offer assistance, and respect any commands the wolf made. No one would question that the wolf just happened to find the bitch out here. By the detective's expression, Rock guessed he was more of a suspect than their brand new pack leader.

The only way to solve this matter would be to do it himself. He turned to Hanson. "Send a few hands out along Hart Highway and see if they find anyone coming off the property at that end."

He turned to look in the direction of his house, not visible over the high meadow grass. Someone could backtrack through the trees, and reenter by the outbuildings. At the moment, he had very few werewolves around his home.

Whoever murdered these three bitches had a motive directed toward him. Of that much, he had no doubt. A fist of frustration gripped his gut, tensing every muscle in his body. He wouldn't allow anyone to hurt Simone. The bitch had too much wild in her. He'd seen the protest in her eyes when he ordered her to stay put. But if she left the house, made herself accessible, and someone was out to hurt him…

"Find Johann Rousseau." He pointed a finger at Hanson, and then at Beuerlein. "Bring him to me."

It would only take a minute or two to get back to the house. He needed to see that she was all right, and that she had obeyed him. He'd lost Dana due to his stupidity, and he wouldn't let it happen again. He needed to protect Simone. He headed back to the house, ignoring the detective calling after him.

"Rock!" Hanson huffed and hobbled after him. "The detective has the pack leader on the phone."

Rock could barely see the roof to his house. Pale blue sky surrounded him, the meadow rising up to meet it. This was land to be proud of, land he wanted to show off to Simone. He wanted to lay her down in the meadow grass and fuck that adorable pussy of hers. He would fight to the last drop of his blood to prevent anyone from taking this from him.

"Where is Johann?" Rock looked in Hanson's direction, and could see Beuerlein standing by the edge of the trees, gesturing for him to come back.

The detective held his cell phone to his ear, obviously talking to someone.

Rock glanced back toward his house, willing his little bitch to be obedient and safe, and then turned and walked back to the detective.

"Johann thinks he knows who it was that he spotted in the woods." The detective clasped his phone to his belt.

"And he didn't tell you?" Rock knew the answer before the detective responded, by the scowl on the wolf's face.

"Actually he did tell me." The detective surprised him with his response. "But I'm going to need a hell of a lot of proof to believe him."

Two werewolves helping the pack doctor, carried the corpse to the van parked in the meadow.

"Since no humans were involved in this murder, and it hasn't been reported to their police station, I can keep this one as pack business." Beuerlein squinted and watched the men load the bitch into the back of the van, then slam the doors closed. "Jordeaux will examine the corpse further after she is taken back to her den."

"Who did Johann say he spotted on my land?" Rock watched the detective study him, not liking the determined look on his face.

"I can't tell you that yet."

Rock wouldn't waste time arguing with the wolf. He would head back to the house, make sure Simone was okay, and then he planned on paying his pack leader a visit. One way or another, the killing would stop.

Chapter Nineteen

Simone kicked her shoes off, and stretched out on the couch. It had taken some effort, but finally the three cubs seemed to be playing nicely together. Nate and Hunter, Rock's cubs, were loaded with spirit and orneriness. There wasn't a bit of doubt in her mind that Rock had sired those two. But they were good boys. Once she told them that Jere would be their new sister, the two had transformed, each one trying to outdo the other impressing her.

The older of the two cubs, and for the life of her she couldn't remember if he were Nate or Hunter, crawled across the living room on all fours, with Jere riding his back.

Now if only Rock would get his adorable ass back home. The kids seemed happy. Quinnie buzzed from room to room cleaning, or doing some chore. Everyone had something to do but her. Although all she wanted to do was Rock. If the werewolf thought she would be a happy mate, staying in his home, and being domestic all day, he would be grossly disappointed.

Being outside appealed to her much better. Maybe she could learn to help him around the ranch. He had Quinnie to help with the cubs, and make the meals. And she seemed to enjoy it. Her place would be with Rock. Now all she had to do was convince him of that.

She left the cubs to their playing, and wandered into the kitchen, staring out the back door, wanting more than anything to explore the outbuildings, see the horses, and explore the land. How long could it take to track down Johann?

She reached for the phone, needing to know what was going on before she went nuts.

"Samantha?" Her friend didn't sound like she was very happy. "Have you talked to Johann recently?"

"I just got off the phone with him. He's on his way home now, and something has him really pissed off."

Simone didn't know what details to offer, but told Samantha what little she knew.

"I'll call you back when I know what's got him pissed." Samantha said her goodbyes. "Oh, wait. Gertrude called too. She's worried about you."

"She doesn't need to worry about me."

"That's what friends do, Simone."

And Simone guessed Gertrude could use a friend. She stared at the phone for a second after hanging up before picking it up again and dialing.

"Yes. Hello." Johann definitely sounded pissed.

"This is Simone." Brief silence followed. She sucked in her breath. "Johann, I hear you found a body on Rock's land."

"Where are you?"

"I'm at Rock's house."

She pulled the phone back when he yelled, "What in the hell are you doing there?"

"We mated, Johann." She couldn't let him take the upper hand with her anymore. "This is where I belong now."

"We'll talk about this later." The background noise silenced, and she guessed he had just turned his car off. "I have other matters to deal with at the moment, as you obviously know."

"We don't need to talk about it later." She reminded herself of Rock's strength, his confidence. She would make her new mate proud, and show the same strength. "Have you seen Rock?"

"No. You don't know where he is?" Samantha spoke in the background now, letting Simone know he was home.

"He left me here to go find you." And if she didn't find out something soon, she would scream.

"Simone." Johann's tone changed, alerting her. "Do you remember Derek Rousseau?"

The question threw her off guard. She came up blank for a moment, not remembering, and not knowing why Johann would ask about him.

The back door opened, startling her. Rock's gaze looked more dangerous than a thunderhead. Concern, frustration, relief all mingled around him, filling the air around her with a mixture of emotions.

"I remember that he was the oldest in his den — Grandmother Rousseau's first-born. He was a prick. Why?"

"Do you remember who he ran with?" Johann's line of questioning made no sense. She didn't remember, and she didn't care.

"No," she managed to say, Rock distracting more than her thoughts. Her pussy seemed to throb on command in his presence.

"Who are you talking to?" Rock didn't stop when he reached her, but pressed her into the counter.

The smell of his emotions mingled with his all-werewolf aroma, making her insides tingle to life. She flattened her hand against his rock-hard chest, feeling his body heat.

"Is that Toubec?" Johann's voice grew louder, and more stern. "Put him on the phone."

Apparently Rock heard Johann because he grabbed the phone from her.

"Whom did you chase across my property?" he yelled into the phone.

He startled her, the spiciness of anger filling the air around them. Her heart skipped a beat from his sudden outburst, and she fought the sensation to sneeze when she breathed in his emotion.

Rock slammed the phone down on the cradle, growling under his breath.

"What is going on?" She'd had about enough of being left in the dark.

Rock noticeably relaxed, releasing a long, slow breath. The brewing storm remained in his eyes, but his expression softened.

"I didn't mean to scare you." He pulled her to him, his hands gripping her waist, and kissed her. It was a quick kiss however, and not with half the feeling of the one he'd given her earlier. "How are you and the cubs doing?"

"They are fine, but I'm not." She tried to push away from him, but his grip tightened. "What did you find out?"

"Nothing." He lifted strands of her hair, then buried his nose in it. "Have Quinnie make all of you a nice meal. I will be home as soon as possible."

"Now where are you going?" Exasperation crept through her. "I don't want to stay here if you're leaving."

"This is your home." His words were hard, obviously misunderstanding her.

"I don't have a problem with that. But I hate being cooped up. I'm going with you." Again she tried to push away from him.

"If you try to leave this house, I swear I will hogtie you, and chain you to the bed."

Any other time she would have come from him saying such a thing, but not now. If she knew one thing about werewolves, it was that they needed to be shown their boundaries. She would not be bullied.

"Look here, Rock Toubec. If you are going after this murderer, then I want to help." She wouldn't be intimidated by the narrowing of his eyebrows, or his lips tightening into an angry, thin line. "Whoever killed those women has disrupted my life as much as yours. And I'm as much a part of this pack as you are. I'm not going to sit back and enjoy a nice supper, while you are out there risking your life."

He pushed her into the kitchen table, but she jumped back to her feet. Tremors threatened her body, but she had to keep her head clear. If this wolf had wanted a docile mate, he shouldn't have chosen her.

Rock straightened, looking down at her. "And what will you do if that murderer captures you, before you capture the murderer?"

Simone sighed, hating it when size and strength were pointed out as necessary traits to get something done.

"Rock. I'm not an idiot." She walked around him, needing her shoes if she were leaving with him. "I wouldn't go chasing after some killer all by myself. But if you are going to go talk to Johann, I'm going too. End of conversation."

Rock didn't say a word, but passed her and walked out the front door. Quinnie had obviously heard their entire conversation, because she assured her the cubs would be fine. As she closed the door behind her, Simone heard Quinnie tell Jere there were some old clothes upstairs, and wouldn't she like to play dress-up?

* * * * *

Rock didn't say a word on the drive into town. It was hard not to sit and fidget, but Simone worried if she started talking, it would be to apologize for standing up to him. And she wasn't in the least bit sorry.

Several other cars were parked outside Johann's house when they arrived.

Rock's fingers wrapped around her wrist when she would have slid out her side of the truck. "When we go in there, I do not want you to be as defiant as you were at the house."

Anger still clouded his eyes, but she couldn't tell if he was angry with her, or the events of the day.

"If you wanted a submissive mate, you chose the wrong bitch." She had no intentions of changing who she was for him.

Rock sighed, and then ran his fingers up her arm. His touch fueled her desire for him, which had never quite ebbed.

"I did not make a mistake in choosing my mate." His tingling touch ran over her shoulder, then his fingers wrapped into her hair. "My instructions are clear. Inside our pack leader's house, you will remain at my side…and quiet."

"But what if…"

"Enough." He didn't let go of her when he opened his door, but pulled her out his side.

You are going to learn some manners, wolf-man.

Simone's stomach twisted in frustrated irritation. When he would have knocked at the door, she reached for the doorknob. She hadn't moved her things out of here yet, and she still had a key. If she hesitated, Rock would see weakness in her. She couldn't deny the bit of relief when Rock said nothing, but followed her into the living room.

Everyone was talking at once.

"I could accept that he killed her, and couldn't get out of sight before you detected him. By the time I got there, I would say she'd been dead for over an hour maybe." The man speaking placed his hand on Gertrude's shoulder. She sat on the arm of the couch, concentrating on her hands in her lap.

She looked up when Simone walked in, her smile not meeting her eyes.

"Speculation." Toby Beuerlein, she recognized him from years past, shook his head. "That doesn't prove he killed her."

"I'm still going to question him." Johann looked more determined than Simone had ever seen him.

He turned when the two of them entered the house, as did the others. Samantha pushed around Johann and grabbed her arm.

"I'm glad you are here," she whispered, and Simone noticed she looked a bit pale.

"Who are you going to question?" Rock moved until he stood in the middle of the living room, the other men giving him room.

Nervous excitement already filled the air in the room. Samantha gripped her arm a bit harder when Johann didn't answer right away, but studied Rock. The two men stared at each other, not blinking, but determining the other's motives, sizing each other up. Tension clogged breathing space as well, making Simone want to jump in the middle of the two wolves, and get to the root of the matter.

Quit playing the tough guy, Johann. Rock isn't the bad guy. She fought to keep her thoughts to herself.

"I'm going to talk to Derek Rousseau." Johann turned his attention to Toby, but Simone could see the tightness of his body, how straight his back was, with his shoulders thrown back. "This is pack business, detective. You may join me if you like, but your badge stays behind. It has no jurisdiction in this matter."

"Derek Rousseau murdered that bitch?" Rock's biceps bulged against his shirt sleeve. Muscles rippled through his chest, stretching his shirt.

Even though his anger mounted, Simone couldn't deny how damned sexy he looked.

"No." Johann waved his hand through the air in front of Rock, a gesture to remain quiet.

Simone sucked in her breath. Johann would be making a grave mistake if he took Rock's presence lightly.

"Then why would you question him?" Rock ignored the gesture. "Who did you chase off of my land, Johann?"

"Armand Gaston."

"You chased Armand?" She couldn't remain quiet. This was all way too confusing. "You chased him, and you couldn't catch him?"

Johann turned to face her, annoyance masking his expression. "I didn't catch him on purpose."

"Why the hell not?" Rock looked ready to pounce.

Johann's expression didn't change when he glanced Rock's way. "Because. Gaston is too much of a wimp to commit a crime like that. He doesn't have the balls to kill a bitch in cold blood. And he is too weak to lift her into a tree and hang her. I wanted to find out whose grudge work the werewolf was doing."

"And he led you to Derek Rousseau?" Rock looked like he was growing angrier by the minute.

"No. But it was Derek's car parked on the highway just beyond the property line. Apparently Gaston used it to take the bitch out there."

"We could see where he dragged her through the woods," Beuerlein added. He turned to the man standing next to Gertrude. "Jordeaux, you are sure she died from hanging?"

"I am sure her neck was broken." Jordeaux adjusted the wire-framed glasses on his nose. "She had some scrapes on her body. I guessed they were from her fighting her attacker. But they could have been made by dragging her through the trees."

"Why did you ask me about Derek Rousseau on the phone?" Simone sensed Rock's disapproving gaze that she hadn't remained silent. But this was making her nuts. She still didn't understand everything. "What does he have to do with all of this?"

"Gaston was driving Rousseau's car. The werewolf has his own car, so there has got to be a reason why he would be in Rousseau's." Johann sighed, running his fingers through his hair, while looking at each of them. "I sent a couple of werewolves over to detain him. I doubt he caused trouble. I suggest you all go home. I'll contact you after I visit with Rousseau."

Rock focused on Johann. Even in his irritation, he made the other werewolves pale in comparison. His sapphire eyes burned deep with emotion, his jaw bone a strong line, pursed with control.

"I'm going with you." He took her arm, guiding them both toward the door.

"Toubec." Johann's tone startled Simone. She turned to see more determination on the wolf's face than she had ever seen before. "I will handle this."

The room silenced. She wanted to reach for Rock when his grasp slid away from her arm. Her mate wasn't a werewolf to be told what to do, or how to handle a matter. He wanted to end the trauma brought on his home, she understood that, but their pack leader had just told him to stand down.

Please don't break into your fur in the middle of the living room.

"Do what you want." Again Rock reached for her, heading for the door.

"Toubec." Johann almost yelled. She could feel the tension ripple through Rock. This time he opened the door, not looking back at Johann. "Toubec. Take your mate home. I will contact you when I know something."

Chapter Twenty

Take your mate home.

In the middle of all the excitement, Simone didn't miss Johann referring to her as Rock's mate. That meant he approved of her choice in a werewolf, and wouldn't challenge it. Rock was hers. Hopefully Johann would dissolve that ridiculous pack law at the next meeting.

"Rock. I'm serious about this." Johann walked up to the truck before Rock could start it. "I don't want you interfering in this."

"I take care of my own. That is not interference." Rock gripped the steering wheel like he would rip it from the dash at any moment.

"If we find the guilty party today." Johann leaned against the open window of the door, dangerously close to Rock. He showed no fear however. And Simone had to admit he might actually turn out to be a decent pack leader. "I know you would kill him the second his confession left his lips."

Rock didn't answer.

"You don't have the right to take pack law into your own hands. If you interfere, I will implement disciplinary action." Johann slapped the truck, straightened, then walked toward his own truck.

Simone sucked in a breath. Reassuring words would not help at the moment.

Rock didn't say a word all the way back to the ranch. He parked out front, then left her, walking around the side of the house, instead of going inside.

Quinnie had the household running smoothly. After checking on Jere, Simone found herself looking out the back door, searching for Rock.

She hadn't really explored the property, other than the large barn she had been held captive in the night she met Rock. So much had happened since that night. And now this was her home, a place to raise Jere. Who would have guessed she would ever have gotten so damned lucky?

"If you're looking for him, he's across the meadow at the cabins." Martin Hanson hobbled passed her, carrying a large saddle. "Not sure he's the best of company though."

He disappeared into the shadows of the barn, leaving her staring in the direction he'd indicated. Tall meadow grass swayed against the breeze. A variety of smells filtered through the air while she walked along the fence. There were no cabins visible, but she could walk that way and see what she found.

By the time she reached the pines bordering the meadow, a row of cabins appeared. They were run down, dilapidated, obviously having seen better days. They would be quite cute if fixed up, and she wondered why Rock hadn't taken the time to do it.

A pile of clothes caught her attention. She sniffed the air, forgetting about the rundown structures.

I'm going to find you, wolf-man.

The sun warmed her back when she pulled off her sweater. The slight breeze puckered her nipples, her breasts looking full and round when she looked down to unbutton her jeans. She kicked off her shoes, then slid her jeans down her legs, fresh air teasing her pussy when she bent over to pull her pants off, and toss them in the pile with Rock's clothes.

No one was around her, but there was still a small thrill in standing naked outside. She trod lightly over the rough ground, barefoot and still human, before triggering that remote sensation deep inside her.

Blood rushed through her veins, her heartbeat increasing, and her senses fine-tuning. Her eyes transformed into that of a werewolf, making the undeveloped area around her change in appearance, and in color. Prickly goose bumps gave her shivers while soft, white fur, the color of the moon, covered her skin. Her body stretched, contorted, the thrill of the beast within her released, creating a ball of excitement in her gut.

She dropped to all fours, and then pranced into the undergrowth surrounded by sweet-smelling pines. How wonderful to be in her fur in the middle of the day, sunlight trickling around the tall trees. She and Jere would become quite spoiled living on this beautiful land.

And I will be even more spoiled enjoying my Cariboo lunewulf.

Now all she had to do was find him.

It had been too long since she ran on Rousseau land, now Toubec land, and she couldn't remember exactly where the property line was. But that proved not to be a problem. Large paw prints, with the fresh smell of dirt where long claws had plowed the ground, created a path she could follow.

Rock had some steam to burn off. She decided to enjoy the same luxury, and burn some steam of her own.

Tearing across the countryside sounded real damned good.

Once the trees were behind her, trampled grass created an easy path to follow. Rock obviously hadn't cared if anyone knew where he headed. Either that, or he was too pissed to give it thought.

Her heart pounded, making her pant so she wouldn't get too hot. The hard sprint got her blood flowing, but Rock must have had quite a lead on her. She still hadn't picked up his scent.

Water sparkled from the sun, inviting her to stop and drink. The small round pond, nestled in the valley, had Rock's paw prints leading right up to it. But there was no Rock.

His tracks disappeared into the water, and even after walking around the pond, she didn't see where they picked back up again.

Well hell.

A low growl gave her chills, causing the hair on her back to stand on end. Water rippled around her paws, just as she noticed the large figure emerge from the water.

Rock stood, water dripping from his coat, making the fur cling to him, and allowing a wonderful view of his muscular frame. Apparently, he had been lying in the water, camouflaging his scent, and preventing her from seeing him. He looked like a deadly beast, rising from the depths, his silver eyes mere slits of glowing aggression. Fur clung to his face, streaking its white color with a darker gray. Long, razor sharp teeth stuck out under his upper lip, adding to his fierce appearance. Whether in fur or in skin, Rock Toubec could be incredibly intimidating.

And she had a feeling that is exactly how he wanted to look. She would not allow her mate to bully, or render fear in her, on any given day, no matter the circumstances. He'd taken a hard blow earlier, with Johann forbidding him to handle matters the way he wished. And she would stand by her mate, supporting him in any way he wished to deal with the situation. But he wouldn't take his irritation out on her. The way he glared at her, she guessed he was in a prime mood to do just that.

Water rippled around him when he moved through it toward her. He lowered his head, his silver eyes seeming to glow with energy as he approached.

It became harder to stay calm with him looking at her like that. Her heart raced in her chest, the pitter-patter making her feel like her whole body vibrated to the beat.

Turmoil brewed in his gaze, but she saw the fire, too. Hot. Dominating. Instinct and human emotions swirling in those predator's eyes.

She side-stepped away from the water, hoping it looked like the moisture annoyed her. But with every second, it became harder to remain calm. As a werewolf, he was almost twice her size. He lowered his head, and his thick, long red tongue moved slowly over his teeth.

Memories of what he could do with that tongue sprang to life. That tongue was any woman's fantasy. Thoughts of him fucking her with it made it hard to stand. Her pussy swelled with primal need, moistening, craving the werewolf who now hovered over her.

She had a perfect view of his cock, which hung like a dangerous weapon between his hind legs. It was as thick as her wrist, and damn near the length of her forearm. The length alone would split her in two, if he could manage to get inside of her.

Rock growled, the rumbling of the guttural sound vibrating through him. He moved alongside her, pressing against her, allowing her to feel the reverberation sink through her skin, teasing her senses, her raw instincts craving his cock.

But we aren't compatible in our fur.

Rational human thoughts warred with her animal instinct, which wanted to fuck. And her human curiosity wasn't helping much either. What would it be like to take on a cock that size?

She took a step backwards, but his head lowered against her rear end, his hard, wet nose pressing against her when she backed into him. Her pussy throbbed, cum seeping through her coat on her inner thighs. The heat between her legs soared to dangerous levels.

She darted forward, being careful not to run into his rear end. His cock was a dangerous temptation, but she knew she couldn't take something that big.

Are you crazy? Do you want to hurt me? She barked at him, stepping backwards while he watched her.

She didn't miss the controlled, possessive look he gave her. Her mouth went dry. Licking her lips didn't help.

And he seemed way too fucking calm. The anger appeared gone. She no longer smelled frustration. No. At the moment, Rock gave her the impression he was very much in control of his actions, and sure of what he wanted.

That thought about brought her heart to her throat. What made matters worse was that try as she would to keep her gaze on his face, that giant cock kept distracting her. What would it be like to be mounted, and pounded, impaled and spread open?

Rock took a step toward her, his long tongue hanging over sharp teeth, making it look like he was grinning at her. She hesitated, his calm aggression distracting her. He moved closer, nuzzling her with his hard head.

The action was gentle, making her lower her defenses, just a little. He had taken her as a mate, pursued her, fought for her. He wouldn't do anything to hurt her.

She swallowed the lump in her throat, and returned the affectionate gesture, pressing her head against his powerful chest. The rumble in his chest let her know her action pleased him. He lifted his giant paw, placing it on her shoulder, and she almost stumbled under the weight.

When she tried to crawl out from under his grip, he dug into her fur with his claws, the pointed ends pressing against her hide. He had her pinned.

She might be able to escape his grasp, and possibly even run from him. But he was twice her size, with twice her speed. If she fought him off any further, he would probably enjoy her efforts, and view it as foreplay.

Her heart pounded with the realization that he was going to fuck her. That incredibly large cock would enter her, and in spite of her rational thought telling her it could do irreversible damage, carnal instinct had her pussy throbbing in anticipation.

His large nose tickled her ear, the length of his tongue smoothing the fur on the side of her head. Warm and moist, he kissed her with slow, long strokes. His paw slid over her shoulder, releasing her from under his weight. He stood over her, kissing her face, licking her fur, sending chills throughout her body.

She remained underneath him, forgetting to try and stand. When she twisted so she could return his affection, she rolled to her side. He licked her neck, his powerful fangs rubbing against her skin, electric chills racing through her. Those almond-shaped silver eyes gazed at her, half-closed, clouded with lust.

She returned his kisses, running her tongue over his coarse coat. But he lowered his head, running that hot, rough tongue of his over her chest. Fire flushed through her, boiling her insides, her pussy throbbing with painful need. Desire overwhelmed her, washing her fears away.

Fuck me, wolf-man.

She rolled to her back, spreading her legs, baring her belly to her mate, submitting to him. A rumble rose deep within him, the sound of pure male satisfaction, glorifying in her admittance to his dominance.

Rock moved lower, his tongue stroking the fur around her pussy. He would make her mad with need, begging to be impaled with his oversized cock.

Oh. Hell yes! She howled with delight when his tongue ran over her swollen pussy. The soothing effect was quickly replaced with longing for him to do it again. That thick tongue moved in and out of her tortured cunt, fucking her, the muscles inside her quivering, tightening with anticipation. He stroked her pussy with his rough tongue, molten heat simmering to a boil. She would burn alive from the inside out, she was sure of it.

Go faster. Damn. Fuck me harder. If her paws were hands, she would grab his head and grind her hips into his face. She wanted him deeper, needed him to stroke every inch of her cunt.

When Rock raised his head, her cum soaked the fur around his mouth. His toothy grin, showing deadly, pointed fangs, would have made her giggle, if she could have made such a sound in her werewolf form. He hovered over her, watching her with silver eyes. His cock throbbed, nodding underneath him, looking very eager for its turn in her cunt. The movement distracted her, reminding her what would happen next. That giant beast would sink inside her cunt.

Rock may have been aware of her fears, but his carnal instinct ran strong. She could see in his expression, the predatory look in his eyes. It was time to fuck her, and his instinct to mate consumed him.

He nipped at her shoulder, pulling her skin with his teeth. *Stand.* His nonverbal command was clear.

She struggled underneath him, her legs reacting like well-worked putty. Human thought grew muddled with werewolf instinct. She would submit to her mate, but he was going to tear her in two.

Her legs barely held her. Her entire body trembled, anticipating a fucking like she'd never known, and terrified at the same time as to what it might do to her.

Her pussy tingled when his cock pressed past her fur, finding the swollen heat that spread inside her, causing the fire within her to burn even more. Pressure built when he pushed against her. How could she stand and take this huge cock penetrating her?

Rock held the nape of her neck with his teeth. Her entrance stretched, working to reach around his massive cock. He pushed, her pussy allowing it, expanding, allowing more and more of him to enter. And still he pushed.

His cock moved inside her, filling her, consuming her, creating wave after wave of desire. Pain mixed with pleasure. He would split her in two. No way could she live through this. Yet, she wanted it more than anything. Wanted him. Wanted his cock, his oversized cock, buried in her small, canine pussy.

Simone buried her claws into the moist dirt underneath her, clamping her jaw shut, determined not to scream. He divided her in two, impaling her while he continued to move deep inside her.

The pressure stretched through her body, a flood of her rich cream threatening to break through her. She would explode if he entered her any further, she just knew it.

But when he began to recede, allowing his cock to flow backward through her cunt, the wall broke, an orgasm rippling through her with more intensity than she had ever experienced. And she was far from a virgin.

The ground moved underneath her, the intensity of her coming made her feel faint. His jaw clamped harder on the back of her neck, the strong pinch of pain mixing with euphoria.

Extreme pleasure, like she'd never experienced before, rushed through her. And just when her mind cleared, when she was able to acknowledge how damned good this felt, he forced his cock deep inside her again.

No longer could she hold back the howls. There was no point in fighting the level of pressure building in her with each thrust. It was moot to question how many times he made her explode. This was fucking on a whole new level. And she loved it.

Rock thrust deep inside her, his movement faster, his actions rougher. She collapsed, unable to stand underneath him any longer. He consumed her, filled her like she'd never been filled before, his cock riding in and out of her. With each thrust, her pussy stretched to meet his size, experience his length, absorb all that he offered.

When he growled, letting her know he was ready to come, everything around her seemed to vibrate. His chest was just above her, his long, thick front legs planted on either side of her, and his growl rumbled through the air around her.

She would pass out. There was no doubt about it. The intensity of him pounding his cock in and out of her was simply too much. She wanted to grab hold of something, anything. Brace herself so that she could maintain his fucking her. Anything to keep from slipping away, pounded by his gigantic cock into a state of oblivion.

His final thrust jabbed her deeper than any cock had ever reached, hitting a point in her womb she never knew could offer such pleasure, making her explode right along with him. Fiery moisture filled her, his seed squirting deep inside her.

Simone couldn't move. Rock's cock quivered inside her, locked deep in her womb. She couldn't even catch her breath. His cock filled her, pressed against her lungs, filled her pussy, consumed every inch of her. The pleasure and pain of her Cariboo *lunewulf* deep within her, claiming every inch of her, brought tears to her eyes.

Emotions she wasn't prepared for flooded through her. There had never been any doubt Rock could fuck her like no other wolf could. And she knew his size would be more than she could handle. But she hadn't been ready for such raw emotions to consume her.

She had mated with her werewolf, with her man, on his land, and in his bed. Bonded for life. His cock, pinning her so that she couldn't move, jerked inside her again, giving her quick chills. And as the chills raced through her, so did another realization. Happiness. Happiness like she had never experienced before. She was stretched wide open, to the point of pain, and she was happy.

Dear God. Was she in love, too? Maybe. She wasn't sure. Something rushed through her, filling her with giddy warmth, bringing tears to her eyes. This was definitely something to think about.

And there was one more thing to think about.

If she could only tame the beast in him…just a bit.

Chapter Twenty-One

Simone didn't want to wake up. Warm comforters cocooned around her, making her warm, and very comfortable. Slowly, her thoughts cleared from a sleepy fog. How long had she slept?

It was almost dark outside. She blinked a few times, noticing Jere sitting cross-legged at the end of Rock's extra-large bed. She had green lace wrapped around her head and neck, and appeared very content studying the contents of an old shoebox.

"Rock said not to wake you." Jere pulled a large marble from the box, and held it up to the light. "I didn't wake you up. You woke up on your own."

The blankets loosened around her when she stretched, causing her to feel the burning deep in her pussy, not to mention fire surging through her inner thigh muscles. Hell. She might as well have just lost her virginity. She was so damned sore.

Memories of Rock carrying her upstairs, insisting she lay on the bed while he drew a hot bath, crept through her mind. At least it didn't hurt to smile. Rock had nestled her into his arms, and lowered her into steaming, scented water. Then he had washed her, stroking every inch of her with luscious suds. She could have stayed in that bath forever.

The bathrobe he had wrapped her in now twisted around her.

Her thoughts faded when voices downstairs crept up toward them.

"Why is Rock mad?" Jere looked at the closed bedroom door, and then stared at her with large, beautiful blue eyes.

Simone could guess what had Rock outraged. She unwrapped herself from the covers, ignoring sore muscles, and found her clothes.

"There is some pack business that has him upset, baby." She pulled her jeans up, and buttoned them. "You haven't done anything wrong."

Jere seemed content with this information. "I didn't wake you up."

Simone opened the bedroom door, Jere by her side with the box of marbles in hand, when a door opened downstairs, then slammed shut. Light from the kitchen flooded into the hallway when she reached the bottom of the stairs.

Before she entered the kitchen, she knew Rock had left. The house seemed oddly quiet, anger dissipating along with the comfortable security she sensed when Rock was around.

"Where did Rock go?" Simone hoped she sounded calm.

Rock's cubs sat at the kitchen table, what was left of a chicken on a plate between them. Jere climbed on to the empty chair, staring at the food anxiously.

"Did you have a nice nap?" Quinnie grabbed what was left of the carcass, and placed it in front of Jere.

She grinned when she faced Simone, a knowing twinkle in her eyes. Apparently, little happened around here without Quinnie knowing about it.

"Yes. Where's Rock?"

The plump bitch gave her the once over, and then turned when the cubs began arguing over what was left of the bird.

"He had a few words for the pack leader, and then stormed out the back door." Quinnie grabbed the older of the two cubs, Nate, if Simone remembered right, and took a towel to his face.

The werewolf took off without her again. She stared at Jere, who stared discontentedly at what was left of the bird carcass.

"How about if we go see Samantha, and see about getting you some supper?"

Jere's grin told Simone that her daughter liked the idea.

She didn't mind running through the back fields with her daughter. The young cub couldn't move as fast in her fur, which was okay, since Simone felt every sore muscle by the time they reached the back yard of her old home.

The kitchen was dark when they entered. She noticed Gertrude sitting on the couch, in the living room. Samantha was talking, but Simone couldn't see her.

"Simone. What are you doing here? Is everything okay?" Gertrude noticed her first.

"Where is Rock?" Samantha appeared in the doorway.

"Hello to you two, also." Simone hid her disappointment that Rock wasn't here. Heat rushed through her, an impending need to find her werewolf, and make sure he wasn't getting into trouble. If he wasn't here, then he must have gone after Johann. "Where is Johann?"

Samantha smiled. "Sounds like neither one of us know where our mate is."

"Samantha was just telling me about Elsa." Gertrude walked into the kitchen, while Samantha busied herself making coffee.

Jere started digging in the refrigerator, lightening the tension Simone felt in the room, when the three women laughed and helped the cub find food.

"Elsa did okay for herself." Simone noticed the sadness in Gertrude's eyes. "Do you miss her?"

"Who? My bratty little sister?" Gertrude laughed, crow's-feet making her look older than Simone knew she was. "I miss both of my sisters sometimes. I miss how simple our lives used to be."

Samantha gave her a sympathetic look, but Simone studied her old friend. "Where is Sophie? Has she left the pack?"

"Oh, no. She and Nik are still here. I just never see much of her."

"How is she doing?" Simone could tell something bothered Gertrude, and she suspected the two of them had been discussing it when she arrived. That would explain the tension she felt.

"Sophie is happy. She has three wonderful mates, and Nik has no problems with either of them coming over from time to time." Gertrude lowered her voice. "Jonathan, one of her mates, has a girlfriend, and she comes over too. I think all of them...well, you know."

Simone couldn't help grinning when Gertrude blushed.

"Sophie is bisexual?" She remembered how excited Sophie had been to fuck all of her mates. "Well, good for her. Sounds like she's made the best of that nasty law Grandmother Rousseau left all of us with."

"A law I know Johann will abolish." Samantha patted Gertrude on the arm.

"I take it life with your three mates isn't going as well?" Simone realized suddenly that might be why her friend worked so much, because her home life sucked.

"That's an understatement." Gertrude stared past Simone, her pretty blue eyes suddenly watery. "Sometimes I think Elsa was the smart one to run."

"The American mate she has now defeated two of her mates in a challenge." Simone took down three coffee cups, and placed them next to the coffeemaker.

"Sounds like everything has worked out well for all of you." Gertrude crossed her arms against her waist, and Simone could see her determination not to cry.

She'd never believed herself any good at consoling someone. It was so hard to know what to say. But her friend's pain was obvious, and Simone had to say something. "I don't remember who your three mates were."

"Matt Jordeaux is one of them. He's our pack doctor." Gertrude shrugged, seeming uncomfortable with the topic. "The other two aren't with the pack anymore."

"You don't like Matt?" Simone wanted to ask why the other two left, but decided Gertrude would tell her if she wanted, and it seemed she was uncomfortable enough talking about any of it.

"We don't talk very much." Gertrude took the cup of coffee Samantha offered, and blew on the hot brew. "He was my first mate. And at first, I thought he was wonderful. When it was time for me to go to my next mate, I couldn't do it. Matthew is sort of possessive."

"Imagine that. A possessive werewolf." Simone rolled her eyes for Gertrude's benefit, happy at least that it brought a smile to her friend's face.

"It's a ridiculous law," Samantha reassured her.

"More milk, Mommy." Jere held her cup up, and Simone took it to the refrigerator.

"It won't be as easy for Johann to dissolve the law as you think." Gertrude nursed her cup of coffee, watching Jere. "There are couples, like Sophie, who are happy having sex with different werewolves."

"Sounds to me like that is a personal matter, between her and Nik." Simone watched Jere gulp down her milk, then climb out of her chair, and disappear down the hall toward their old bedroom. "Dissolving that law won't disturb their happiness."

Simone couldn't picture Rock being willing to share her with another werewolf. If his behavior toward Armand Gaston were any indication, she would never have to worry about another werewolf bothering her. Rock would always be possessive of her, which didn't bother her a bit. What a change from the casual fucks she had known for so many years. None of them cared at all what she did the next day.

That thought made her wonder again where he might be. If he had returned to the house, he would be looking for her. She suspected this would be the first place he would look. But she had a feeling he wasn't home. More than likely, he had taken off after Johann.

Quinnie had told her that Rock had words with Johann over the phone, and had stormed out of the house right after that. If he had gone to Derek Rousseau's house, it would be real hard for anyone to prevent him from taking matters into his own hands.

"Simone?" Samantha brought her out of her meanderings. "Thinking about Rock, are you?"

She sighed when both Samantha and Gertrude gave each other knowing looks.

"Yeah, actually I was. I'm worried he will get himself into trouble. Rock won't listen to Johann." She didn't want to offend Samantha, but it was the truth. She doubted the werewolf would listen to anyone.

"There were many who wanted Rock to be pack leader," Gertrude told them. "The Rousseaus threw a fit, and then announced loudly when they found Johann and he agreed to return home. They wanted the pack leader to remain in the Rousseau family."

"He's Cariboo *lunewulf*. That would have caused all kinds of problems with this uptight pack." Simone could only imagine the reaction many would have had if Rock had become leader.

He would make an outstanding pack leader. But he would have ruled with an iron hand. Johann was more of the diplomat, and maybe that was what this pack needed to get back on to its feet.

It was a good thing Rock wasn't pack leader. She liked having him to herself, and with all that room on his ranch, they would have plenty of privacy.

"He has a lot of respect in the pack." Gertrude pulled her from her thoughts once again. "You got yourself a good mate."

"Yeah, I do." She couldn't argue that one. "But I'm dying to know where the hell he is right now."

Causing trouble, she feared. The more she thought about it, the more she needed to go find him. He would kill whoever murdered those bitches. She didn't doubt that for a second.

And if Johann brought pack law down on Rock for killing a murderer…

That thought made her sick to her stomach. She knew the two werewolves already barely got along. And as pack leader, Johann could kill Rock for murdering another werewolf, even if the wolf were a murderer.

What was she thinking? Johann wouldn't be able to kill Rock. Her werewolf was undefeatable. But Johann could make his life hell for him. Johann could have Rock shunned, preventing any merchant from doing business with him. What a mess that would be. The more she thought about it, the more she knew she needed to find Rock, and prevent him from doing anything rash.

"I need to go find him," she blurted out, before she had even figured out how she would stop him from doing anything he had set his mind to doing.

"And what are you going to do if you find him?" Samantha was queen bitch. Simone realized she could order her not to leave.

"I'm not sure." She really didn't have a set plan. "Maybe if he sees me, it will distract him from any plan he may have."

Samantha didn't look convinced. She glanced at Gertrude, who watched her as well. Then she placed her hands on the bulge in her tummy, and sighed.

"Okay. One hour. But you better check in with me within the hour, okay?"

* * * * *

Simone rubbed at the wet spot that had formed on her shirt from carrying it in her mouth. She really needed to get a car. Getting from one place to another in her fur wasn't a problem, but after a while, her clothes got wrinkled…and damp.

It had surprised her a bit to see Derek Rousseau's house dark and quiet. No one had been home. But it surprised her even more to find Rock's truck parked outside Howley's, and Johann's Suburban there as well.

"Now what to do." She paced outside the front of the bar, muttering to herself, trying to figure out the best approach. She hadn't expected Johann to be with Rock.

There were more cars parked along the street. She didn't recognize any of them, but it seemed a lot of people were inside Howley's. Images of storming the bar and grill, only to run straight into the iron chest of Rock, didn't sound like it would accomplish much. Well possibly she would find herself strapped to his truck.

No. She needed to learn what they were up to, without being obvious. How would she enter Howley's without every head turning to see her do so?

The front door to the bar and grill almost hit her in the nose when someone pushed it open while she paced.

"Excuse me." Jordan Rousseau stepped around the open door, but then halted when he recognized her. "Well, well. Simone De Beaux."

"It's Simone Toubec." She didn't like the way Jordan's beady eyes undressed her.

He let the door to Howley's close behind him, the noise and smells of the bar and grill fading quickly. Unease settled around her.

"So you have mated with the Cariboo?" Jordan moved to pass, but then turned, facing her. "But could such a mating be legal?"

The best thing to do would be to make it look like she was headed to Rock's truck. There was no reason to respond. She didn't answer to him, or anyone else.

"Now where are you going?" Jordan moved again, blocking her path. "I do believe your Cariboo mate, legitimate or not, is inside. But you are not joining him? Could it be he doesn't know you are out here?"

She didn't like the emotions swirling in the air. Jordan stood a fair bit taller than she, but he was skinny, no muscle to speak of. It wouldn't be too hard to bully him. However, a warped sense of determination swirled around the werewolf, making her nervous.

"Move, wolf-man." She put her hands on her hips, glaring at him.

"Or what? You'll kick my ass?" He snorted, a most unappealing sound. "From what I hear of you, your best work is on your back."

"My best work is any position I choose." She wanted to smack that pompous expression right off his face. Who the hell did he think he was? "And yeah, right now I could do very good work kicking your ass."

She didn't expect aggression out of him. His blue eyes seemed to glaze with fury. He moved faster than she expected, wrapping his long bony fingers around her neck.

"I've had enough threats for one night," he hissed. His spit hit her in the face, making her stomach turn. "The last thing I need is the likes of you, slut, trying to bully me."

"Get your hands off of me." She pried at his fingers, wrapped around her neck, but he grabbed her wrist, and pushed her backwards.

The door to Howley's opened again. He tried to push her into the alcove of the nearest store, stealing the shadows for shelter. He surprised her with his strength, obviously fueled by anger. The best she could do was to keep them at a standstill.

"What are you doing?" Matthew, Gertrude's mate, stopped, noticing the two of them.

"Let go of me, you scrawny mutt." Simone could have kissed Matthew for his timely arrival. Not that she needed any help. "You're going to make a fool out of yourself."

"You breed with a Cariboo, and call me a mutt?" Jordan's grip around her neck tightened, making it hard to breathe. "God only knows how many mutts you have fucked, you disgraceful slut."

"You know. She might just be the answer to our problems." Matthew tapped his chin, studying her, a quiet calm in his tone that chilled Simone's blood. "We can do this murder ourselves, and make sure it looks like Toubec did it. Then Johann would definitely run him out of town."

Jordan must be blocking air to her brain. What had Matthew just said? And why did he stand there calmly watching her, when this scrawny werewolf had his fingers around her neck.

"Let me go!" It was a struggle to speak. Breathing became difficult. She could feel her fingernails dig into Jordan's flesh, with her efforts to make him release her.

"That's exactly what I was just thinking." Jordan shoved her against the brick wall behind her. "Toubec sits in that bar like he owns the place. And he has some of the merchants backing him now. But this little bitch here will ensure that everyone hates Toubec. No longer will he have the support of the pack."

It scraped her back, banged the back of her head. Realization hit her that she could be in trouble, and she kicked with all her might, rejoicing when the tip of her boot hit a bone.

"Bitch!" Jordan spit in her face again.

"My car is right here. Let's get her out of here before we are noticed." Matthew reached out, grabbed her nipple through her shirt, and twisted it painfully. "You, little bitch-slut, have just become our meal ticket."

She put everything she had into fighting them. She kicked, managed to free her hands and struck out. She even tried changing in the middle of downtown, purely out of desperation. Halfway through the change, from woman to beast, something sharp pricked her shoulder. The last thing she saw before blackness consumed her was Matthew, with a needle in his hand, injecting something into her flesh. His expression was pure evil.

Chapter Twenty-Two

Everything was blurry. Simone pried her tongue from the top of her mouth, and realized she was dying of thirst. The room seemed to spin when she forced herself to sit.

Where the hell was she? She jumped at the sound of thunder, and then the crack of lightning, which briefly lit the dark room she was in. Recent memories flooded through her just as a torrent of rain pelted the window.

Matthew, the pack doctor, and Jordan, one of the established Rousseaus, had kidnapped her. It took a moment to get her bearings when she stood, and she leaned the back of her legs against the bed until she got her head together. It made no sense why they had taken her, or the last words she remembered them saying before she passed out.

"How am I an answer to a problem?" Her voice cracked, and she coughed. "And what was that about a meal ticket?"

The rain made it hard to see out the window. Everything was pitch-dark. She pressed her face to the cool glass, doing her best to identify the surroundings outside. All she saw was trees, and the fact that she was in an upstairs bedroom. So much for changing, and running through the window.

"He'll go for it. I'm confident of the fact."

She spun around at the sound of voices outside the bedroom door.

"I heard he about attacked Gaston down at Howley's for touching the little slut." Jordan Rousseau chuckled.

There was other men's laughter too.

"Those Cariboo get mighty possessive of their own. They will attack without notice." Matthew's voice sounded nearer. "They are a completely unpredictable species."

Simone crept across the room, moving as quietly as she could until she leaned against the wall next to the door.

"Which is just another example of how unstable their hybrid breeding is. Grandmother wasn't thinking clearly when she stated the Cariboo were equal in breeding to the pure *lunewulf*. They are obviously quite primitive compared to us." Derek Rousseau allowed enough hatred to swirl around his words that she swore she could smell it through the walls.

Her heart pounded so hard she could hardly hear. They were right outside the bedroom door. She searched the dark room, clueless what to do when they entered. And she was scared to death that they would open that door any minute.

"Claiming to be with that slut in there won't hold as an alibi." Jordan's laughter twisted her stomach. "The pack doesn't trust him now. They will push Johann to run him out of town. We will be able to pin the murders on him. And if we can't, a private bargain with the Cariboo should do the trick."

"Then gentlemen, our work will be done." Derek Rousseau sounded so damned arrogant she fought the urge not to pull the door open, and yell in his face. "We will notify Toubec that he may have his slut back alive after we are assured he has left town. But first, shall we enjoy the spoils of our hard work?"

Light flooded the room when the door opened. It took only a second for Simone to understand the meaning of Derek's words. She was the spoils. But she would be damned if they would enjoy her for one second.

"Where the hell is she?" Matthew's fury, as he stared at the rumpled covers on the bed she had been on, gave her chills.

Someone turned on the bedroom light, stealing the darkness that protected her. Before anyone could notice her, she charged into Derek, hitting him square in the back.

"You will all die for this," she screamed, while she and Derek tumbled to the floor.

There were only seconds. The chances of her taking down three werewolves were slim to none. But she had to give it her best shot. Her knuckles crushed into Derek's ear. His screams fed her strength.

"Fucking little bitch." Matthew grabbed her, lifting her off the ground.

She only got a second to see Derek lying on the ground, moaning, while holding his head. But it was a wonderful moment of satisfaction.

Jordan slapped her hard across the face, making her bite her tongue, while stars sparkled in front of her vision.

Thunder vibrated the house, and lightning lit the windows briefly, like two giant eyes blinking at her.

"Get her out of her clothes. I deserve to fuck her first." Derek Rousseau struggled to stand, still holding the side of his head.

"None of you bastards will fuck me." She twisted with all the strength she had, almost knocking her and Matthew to the ground. "You will all rot in hell for this."

Jordan slapped her again. The entire side of her face stung with so much pain she almost couldn't feel it. Her eyes watered too much to see. But she could feel the hands on her. Everything seemed to swim around in her head. She couldn't tell if she was standing or not, but hands continued to paw at her, she knew that much.

"Just pull her shirt over her head," Matthew was saying. His words sounded like they came through a tunnel. "No need to take it off of the slut. It will serve to blindfold her, and immobilize her arms. Pin her down while she is still disoriented."

No. Please. Did she speak out loud, or only in her thoughts? *Shit. Don't rape me.*

In all her years of promiscuity, she had never been raped. She had enjoyed group sex, gangbangs, one-night stands. But no one had ever taken her by force. This couldn't be happening.

Her heart lurched in her chest when she realized someone sucked on one of her nipples. Bruising hands twisted and pulled on her breasts. Her vision wouldn't clear. She tried to rub her eyes, and ignore the teeth that scraped her nipples, but her arms seemed all twisted in something.

Her shirt. Her arms were twisted in her shirt, which had been pulled over her head. She almost panicked in her efforts to pull the shirt off of her the rest of the way.

"I knew you would come around, you nasty slut." Matthew's breath burned her flesh. "Everyone knows you will fuck any werewolf who howls at you."

She threw her shirt to the side, then elbowed the pack doctor as hard as she could in the chest. He had his arms wrapped around her, and Jordan mauled at her breasts. The buttons on the fly of her jeans sprang free at the same time that Jordan bit one of her nipples.

"Oww!" She howled, the pain in her nipple racing through her.

"Every time you try to hurt one of us, we will hurt you." Jordan leered at her. "Do you like pain, Simone?"

"Fuck you." She spit in his face.

Her jeans slid down her legs, almost knocking her off balance. Matthew didn't bother to try and pull them off of her, but let them tangle around her knees, and ankles.

"Oh, hell yes." Derek managed to stand now, his hand barely covering a nasty green-blue bruise that spread along the side of his face. "I just love a shaved pussy."

She was outnumbered. At the rate things were going, she would have the old bastard's dick inside her within minutes, assuming he could still get it up. Her options were grossly limited, but she had no choice.

The change rippled through her, and she glorified in the strength, and power, that the beast within her allowed. Before any of them could react, she lunged forward, biting Jordan in the face. Blood filled her mouth, his howls echoing through the room.

She twisted free of Matthew, and bolted out of the bedroom, clueless as to how far she could get before they would catch her again.

* * * * *

Rock had just about had enough of this bullshit. Nothing was getting accomplished here. Johann had managed to get half of the pack riled, and the lot of them stood inside Howley's, arguing over how best to handle the situation.

He needed to get out of here, get some fresh air. Too many people involved would only allow for mistakes anyway. Johann worked to keep the handful of werewolves, who had learned of the third murder and demanded action, satisfied with answers.

Rock threw a bill down on the table, deciding to take another drive out to Derek Rousseau's place. Or maybe he would drop in and pay Armand Gaston a visit.

He headed for the door, then noticed Johann staring at him while talking on his cell phone.

"When did you last see her?" For some reason, the sudden anger in the pack leader's tone, alerted him. "Well, why the hell did you let her go out on her own?"

Something was wrong. Rock sensed it immediately. Johann turned away from the group, heading for the door, still talking on his cell phone. Rock caught the door before it closed behind Johann.

"Calm down. It's okay. I'm sorry." Johann headed toward his truck, but then stopped, possibly sensing that Rock was behind him. He turned around, frustration apparent in his expression. "What time did she leave?" The wolf nodded, watching him. "Did she say where she was going?" Johann sighed. "Well she didn't find him. He's standing right here in front of me."

Simone. Something was wrong with Simone. A clamp pressed against his heart. Rock didn't like the sound of this. He would dismember any werewolf who might bring Simone trouble. The hell with pack law.

"Don't worry. We'll find her." Johann hung up the phone. His expression was hard when he returned Rock's stare. "Simone showed up at my house over an hour ago. Samantha allowed her to take off looking for you, but she had instructions to check in after an hour, and she didn't do it."

"Damnit." Rock headed toward his truck.

"Where are you going?" Johann was parked nearby, and headed for his truck too. "She should have been able to find you, Toubec."

"Which means something happened to her." Rock pulled his truck door open, but then turned when Johann called out to him.

"Don't take off without a plan. You'll tell me where you are going."

Rock saw concern in the werewolf's eyes, but couldn't determine the wolf's motives. "I have a plan. I will find her, and if she's been harmed, whoever did it shall die."

He didn't look toward the werewolf again until he had his truck running. "And what would you do if you found her in a bad situation?"

"Probably the same thing you would." Johann climbed into his Suburban, and then gestured for Rock to lead the way.

Rock couldn't help but wonder if Johann would be upset enough to kill any wolf who wronged a woman, or if his feelings for Simone went deeper than just a concerned pack leader.

He didn't give thought to where he drove. Instead memories of Dana popped into his head. Now was not the time to dwell on his first mate. What happened to her would not happen to Simone. But he couldn't get the thoughts to go away. His free-spirited first mate had thought she could take on the world all by herself. And damnit to hell if he hadn't found another mate with that same willful spirit.

Derek Rousseau's house appeared ahead before he realized he had driven there. He pulled into the circular drive, and cut the headlights.

"Something isn't right." Johann walked up next to him, after parking his Suburban on the other side of a sedan that Rock didn't recognize.

"Derek's car, and one other are parked out front, but there are no lights on." Rock didn't like the looks of it either.

He didn't care if his boots crunched over the gravel as he headed around the outside of the house. Rock had no intention of keeping his presence here a secret.

"There's a light on upstairs." Johann pointed toward an upstairs window.

They rounded the back of the house at the same time glass crashing stopped him in his tracks.

"What the fuck?" Johann stopped next to him.

Glass barely missed him. Rock jumped to the side just as a white blur flew out of a downstairs window.

He had never understood the nature of a werewolf who would want to live in town. But Derek Rousseau had a nice suburban home. In fact, most of the Rousseaus lived in town, which probably explained why they were such an uptight lot.

Several neighborhood dogs started barking ferociously. If they weren't careful, concerned humans would be all over the place in no time. The last thing he wanted was humans poking their nose into his business.

It only took a second to recognize Simone. She rolled across the grass, then found her footing and shook glass free of her silver-white coat. Then she noticed him.

"What the hell do you think you are doing?" He started toward her, focusing on those almond-shaped, silver eyes that glowed at him in the dark.

"There are more inside." Johann grabbed his arm, and he fought the impulse to shake the werewolf off of him.

Fury and confusion warred inside him. Whoever was in the house wouldn't get far. And something had terrified Simone enough to make her change into her fur in the middle of town, and jump out of the window of a house.

He pulled his shirt over his head. "Change," he yelled at her, and held the shirt out to cover her.

She looked just as wild in her human form as she had in her fur. He pulled his shirt over her head, noticing that the side of her face looked bruised.

"What the hell happened to you?" Johann walked around him, apparently indifferent to the fact that Rock tried to shield her nudity from him.

"Derek. Jordan. Matthew." She pointed a shaky finger toward the house. "Don't let them get away."

Rock had no intention of allowing any wolf to escape who had put his mate into such a state of shock.

Johann already headed toward the back door when the sound of a car starting out front made him stop in his tracks.

Rock heard Simone cry out but didn't have time to listen to her attempt at giving instructions. He raced after the car that had just turned on its headlights, backing up to make room to get around his truck. Rock jumped over the hood, feeling the metal give way under his boot. He had the driver's side door handle in his grip before the driver could put the car in drive.

Simone had cried out three names, and three werewolves were in the car. That was good enough for him. Answers could come later. Right now they would pay for the condition in which he had just found his mate.

"Rock. No!" Johann's order seemed to come through a dense fog. "Put the werewolf down. I want answers before you kill him."

Rock stared into the terrified eyes of Derek Rousseau, who made a feeble attempt to stop his neck from being broken.

Chapter Twenty-Three

The sun soaked through her skin, and Simone shielded her eyes against it when she turned to wait for Samantha and Johann to catch up.

"You are going to love this. It's the perfect little hideaway." She grinned when Samantha smiled at her.

Rock wrapped his arm around her waist, his steely body pressing against her backside. His hand slipped under her shirt, tweaking a nipple shamelessly.

"I love you," he whispered into her ear, his hot breath spreading through her like an aphrodisiac.

She turned in his arms, indifferent to Gertrude, who stood next to them, and stretched against him, wrapping her arms around his neck.

"I love you, too." She'd never told a werewolf that before, not even Johann. But the emotions that surged through her right now were new, and she had no doubt about her feelings.

"If you two make the air smell any thicker, you're going to make me horny," Gertrude teased next to them.

Rock didn't let her go, but kissed her forehead. She rested her cheek against his chest, and smiled at her friend.

Gertrude looked noticeably better over the past couple of days. After the nightmare ended, and the punishments were carried out, she had invited Gertrude to stay with them. They had enjoyed a few days of laziness, and today had invited Samantha and Johann out for a day on the ranch.

"They are right over here." Rock released her, but then took her hand in his, while leading them toward the row of cabins.

"They kind of remind me of the cabins Elsa and Rick were building when we left." Samantha leaned against Johann, the sunlight making her appear radiant.

"Rock wants to refurbish them, and make a retreat for the pack out here." Simone was so proud of her mate for wanting to share this beautiful land with everyone.

"I wouldn't be surprised if you get a lot of volunteers to help you with the project." Johann looked over her at Rock. "It was pretty clear the other night at the impromptu pack meeting that the majority of the pack doesn't feel the way the few Rousseaus felt."

"We're Rousseaus." Gertrude punched his arm playfully. "Don't let those uptight bastards bring down our good name."

Johann smiled. "I never did buy into their belief that the color of our fur made us any better than other werewolves."

"If anyone needs work," Rock stared at the row of cabins, "I will pay good wages to get these cabins fixed up."

"I'll announce it at the next pack meeting." Johann's expression turned serious. "It was obvious the other night that you have the respect of most of the pack already. No one denied you your right to end those three werewolves' lives."

A crashing sound came from the trees, and Simone turned to watch her daughter tearing through the underbrush, chasing Nate and Hunter. The cubs ignored the group of adults, and ran toward the cabins.

"She's going to be as wild as her mother." Johann shook his head, but the pride in his expression was noticeable.

"I might have to get collars and leashes for both of them." Rock pulled her back into his arms, the heat of his body wrapping around her.

"You do and I'll use them on you." Simone squirmed in his grasp, taking pleasure in feeling his cock harden against her lower back.

"Cariboo *lunewulf* do not take nicely to being put on a leash." His breath spread heat down the side of her face.

She wondered when her next opportunity to ride his cock would be.

Johann turned his attention to Rock, his expression turning grave. "You don't have to worry about your breed."

"I'm not worried." Rock let go of her, turning toward the cabins.

She followed him, realizing the conversation would turn serious. She craved his touch again, although she didn't touch him when he stopped to survey the siding on the nearest cabin.

"Do you think there will be more trouble with the pack?" Johann opened the door to the cabin, disappearing inside.

"Matthew Jordeaux, Derek Rousseau and Jordan Rousseau are dead." Rock offered no emotion, although she knew he found little pleasure in breaking their necks.

"And Armand Gaston fled the pack," Johann added. "I've notified the pack south of Prince George. He'll be shunned wherever he goes."

Rock lowered his head to enter the cabin. She followed, with Samantha behind her. The cabins would be absolutely adorable with a little elbow grease, and some fixing up.

"Everyone else in the pack respects you." She couldn't keep her hands off him. Her pussy throbbed when he grinned down at her, while wrapping his fingers through her hair.

"And they will respect you, too." His lips brushed over hers, smoldering her insides.

Samantha and Johann spent the rest of the afternoon visiting, leaving before supper when Samantha started showing signs of fatigue. Gertrude and Jere left with them. Simone knew Gertrude felt awkward staying with her, after learning her mate had attempted to rape her. But Simone had reassured her that she knew Gertrude had nothing to do with it.

Even so, she could still see the ghosts haunting her friend in her masked expression. It would take a while for Gertrude to get accustomed to being a single bitch again, and to get over the fact that her mate had been involved in the murders of three innocent females.

Simone took her time walking down the large hallway, after making sure Nate and Hunter slept soundly in their beds. Her thoughts drifted, while she stared at the framed pictures on the wall of Rock's family members. Rock, too, believed in strong family ties, and the strength of his heritage. But unlike the founding members of this pack, he judged a werewolf by their abilities. She still marveled over how good of a catch she had found for herself. If she was dreaming, the last thing she ever wanted to do was wake up.

"Get your ass in here, bitch of mine." Rock's growl made her pussy pulsate with instant need.

She pushed the door to their bedroom open, and grinned at the naked werewolf sprawled on their bed, his cock in his hand.

"When I say come, I expect you to move." His expression was serious, and she didn't doubt for a second that he meant every word he said.

"I'll come when I damn well feel like it." She leaned against the doorway, crossing her arms.

He sprung from the bed, muscles rippling in his chest and legs. She had no desire to move, but simply enjoyed the wonderful view. His cock remained hard and erect while he moved in on her.

Large hands, with so much power, yet the ability to be amazingly gentle, moved over her sensitive breasts, and then grabbed her under the arms, lifting her until she stared head on into those beautiful sapphire eyes. His beard was still damp from his shower, almost red as it clung to the curve of his strong chin.

"You will learn to obey me." He pushed her up against the wall.

She had no doubt she would, with such a sexy teacher. She wrapped her legs around his waist, her black slip sliding up to expose her pussy. Rock didn't hesitate, but pushed his cock against the heat of her swollen entrance, until he glided deep inside her cunt.

"You are already learning to obey me." Pressure climbed to a dangerous point, his cock buried so deep inside her she wanted to scream. It took several long, deep breaths before she could continue to taunt him. "Already you are right where I want you."

His hips rocked against her legs. That massive cock moved easily against the moist inner walls of her pussy, the movement making her juices flow, and stealing her breath. She clung to his shoulders, her fingers pressing hard against his smooth muscles.

"Am I, now?" Mischief sparkled in his eyes, and he thrust his cock deep inside her again.

The back of her head hit the wall, although she barely noticed. Fireworks exploded inside her, colors splashing in front of her eyes. She swore his cock plunged inside her clear to her bellybutton. A dam broke inside her, wave after wave of incredible heat and passion pouring through her.

"Oh yes," she managed to say with some effort. "You seem to train quite nicely."

"I'm glad you approve." He pulled back, then tore into her again, pulling her away from the wall this time, one hand sliding down her back to her ass, and holding her in place. "I, on the other hand, fear I am going to have to spend the rest of my life taming you."

He fell on to the bed, holding her to him. She yelped when his cock bounced back, just to plunge once again into her pussy.

"That sounds just fine with me." She used all the strength she could muster to tighten her pussy muscles around his cock, wanting nothing more than to keep him buried inside her forever. "This might just take a lifetime."

About the author:

All my life, I've wondered at how people fall into the routines of life. The paths we travel seemed to be well-trodden by society. We go to school, fall in love, find a line of work (and hope and pray it is one we like), have children and do our best to mold them into good people who will travel the same path. This is the path so commonly referred to as the "real world".

The characters in my books are destined to stray down a different path other than the one society suggests. Each story leads the reader into a world altered slightly from the one they know. For me, this is what good fiction is about, an opportunity to escape from the daily grind and wander down someone else's path.

Lorie O'Clare lives in Kansas with her three sons.

Lorie O'Clare welcomes mail from readers. You can write to her c/o Ellora's Cave Publishing at 1337 Commerce Drive, Suite 13, Stow OH 44224.

Why an electronic book?

We live in the Information Age—an exciting time in the history of human civilization in which technology rules supreme and continues to progress in leaps and bounds every minute of every hour of every day. For a multitude of reasons, more and more avid literary fans are opting to purchase e-books instead of paperbacks. The question to those not yet initiated to the world of electronic reading is simply: *why?*

1. *Price.* An electronic title at Ellora's Cave Publishing runs anywhere from 40-75% less than the cover price of the <u>exact same title</u> in paperback format. Why? Cold mathematics. It is less expensive to publish an e-book than it is to publish a paperback, so the savings are passed along to the consumer.

2. *Space.* Running out of room to house your paperback books? That is one worry you will never have with electronic novels. For a low one-time cost, you can purchase a handheld computer designed specifically for e-reading purposes. Many e-readers are larger than the average handheld, giving you plenty of screen room. Better yet, hundreds of titles can be stored within your new library—a single microchip. (Please note that Ellora's Cave does not endorse any specific brands. You can check our website at www.ellorascave.com for customer recommendations we make available to new consumers.)

3. *Mobility.* Because your new library now consists of only a microchip, your entire cache of books can be taken with you wherever you go.

4. *Personal preferences are accounted for.* Are the words you are currently reading too small? Too large? Too...**ANNOYING**? Paperback books cannot be modified according to personal preferences, but e-books can.

5. *Innovation.* The way you read a book is not the only advancement the Information Age has gifted the literary community with. There is also the factor of what you can read. Ellora's Cave Publishing will be introducing a new line of interactive titles that are available in e-book format only.

6. *Instant gratification.* Is it the middle of the night and all the bookstores are closed? Are you tired of waiting days—sometimes weeks—for online and offline bookstores to ship the novels you bought? Ellora's Cave Publishing sells instantaneous downloads 24 hours a day, 7 days a week, 365 days a year. Our e-book delivery system is 100% automated, meaning your order is filled as soon as you pay for it.

Those are a few of the top reasons why electronic novels are displacing paperbacks for many an avid reader. As always, Ellora's Cave Publishing welcomes your questions and comments. We invite you to email us at service@ellorascave.com or write to us directly at: 1337 Commerce Drive, Suite 13, Stow OH 44224.

Discover for yourself why readers can't get enough of the multiple award-winning publisher Ellora's Cave. Whether you prefer e-books or paperbacks, be sure to visit EC on the web at www.ellorascave.com for an erotic reading experience that will leave you breathless.

WWW.ELLORASCAVE.COM

Printed in the United States
28478LVS00003BA/61-708